# COPS GONE BAD

## An A. J. Hawke Legal Thriller

## Donald E. McInnis

J&E Publications
San Diego, California

Published by
J & E Publications
www.donaldmcinnis.com

ISBN: 979-8-9865516-6-1

Library of Congress Control Number: 2024916628

Cover design by Timothy W. Brittain

Printed in the United States of America

# Praise for *Cops Gone Bad*

**Cops Gone Bad**, *centering on a young, ambitious lawyer who unmasks a conspiracy within law enforcement, delivers with brisk action and high stakes.*

—Publisher's Weekly Booklife Review

*Readers who choose this legal thriller will find its cat-and-mouse moves offer windows into corruption and law enforcement quandaries.*

*As secrets, surveillance, and scary moments evolve, A.J. finds additional tests to his legal and ethical prowess that both educate him and move him into threatening new directions.*

*McInnis builds a close inspection of how justice can be thwarted and warped. The tension and characterization are well done, but especially notable are themes that run through the plot to provide food for thought to individuals and discussion groups interested in legal processes and precedents.*

**Cops Gone Bad** *is filled with action and insight, and perfect for patrons interested in more than courtroom proceedings, but bigger-picture thinking about social issues, justice, and criminal definitions.*

—Midwest Book Review

# A.J. Hawke Legal Thrillers
# by Donald E. McInnis

### The Sphynx Murder Case

*McInnis infuses the intrigue of ongoing investigations with the suspense of courtroom proceedings. Lawyer A.J. Hawke is clever and crafty in the courtroom as he exposes police interrogation tactics.*

—Publisher's Weekly Booklife Report

### Return of The Sphynx

*Editor's Choice — Nail-biting legal thriller. In this second book of the series, scrappy lawyer A.J. Hawke must use sophisticated science, and his fists, to aid a client. Great for fans of Scott Turow, Phillip Margolin.*

—Publisher's Weekly Booklife Reviews

### Blood of the Father

*"Highly recommended"*—Blood of the Father *is a legal thriller filled with rare, vibrant descriptions that will especially resonate with readers already familiar with the legal system. Few authors are in a position to as realistically portray the challenges of being a lawyer as lawyer/author Donald E. McInnis.*

—Midwest Book Review

# Nonfiction by Donald E. McInnis

*She's So Cold: The Stephanie Crowe Murder Case—*

*A Defense Attorney's Inside Story*

In this true-crime account, Donald E. McInnis unveils the truth behind the coerced confessions that nearly sent three innocent 14-year-old boys to prison for a crime they did not commit.

*A powerful read. . . . Donald E. McInnis does an outstanding job of pinpointing the problems of juvenile prosecution methods. . . . No reader of true crime or juvenile rights should be without this outstanding book. . . . Law professors will find* She's So Cold [second edition] *holds much fodder for classroom discussion and debate.*

—Midwest Book Review

**Reader reviews:**

*It was never going to be rated anything BUT five stars! . . . An absolutely fantastic read. Up there with* In Cold Blood *by Truman Capote. I enjoyed it THAT much.*

—Yassemin T, NetGalley

*If you enjoy mysteries you will love this. If you want to see why we need more people like Donald McInnis working for us, you will enjoy this. . . . Mr. McInnis does a wonderful job of laying out the facts without prejudice. He simply states what happened. Fascinating read!*

—Maria's Space

She So Cold *is one of the most harrowing stories I have read. . . . This is a gripping tale of law enforcement gone lawless.*

—English Plus Blog

For more reviews and internet interviews regarding Donald E. McInnis's representation of one of the 14-year-old boys, go to: donaldmcinnis.com.

# AUTHOR'S NOTE

Once again, our young lawyer Andrew Jackson "Drew" Hawke finds himself deeply embroiled in another aspect of the legal system. This time he faces something few people talk about: The police brotherhood and its Blue Code of Silence.

For most of English history, not all antisocial or even minor criminal acts made it into the court system. In older times, the local beat constable decided which conduct the legal system would prosecute. Offenders of minor offenses were given a warning by the officer. Young men were taken home to be disciplined by parents rather than arrested or brought before a magistrate.

The English term misdemeanor is derived from the Latin *minari*. By the 14$^{th}$ century, English-speaking people had changed this Latin phrase to the word *demean*: to conduct or behave in a proper manner or, as time passed, behavior toward others. Misdemeanor meant to act improperly or behave wrongly. Somehow such misbehaving conduct started finding its way more and more into the criminal court system as society tried to regulate citizen conduct, not through the pressures of the family or society, but by criminal punishments.

In writing this story, I try to illustrate the need for our society to be vigilant about the cornerstone of all societies' justice systems—the law enforcement officers. They are the ones who interreact with the citizenry. How the police treat their fellow citizens determines how strong the bond is between those that need and praise law enforcement officers as opposed to those who fear or hate them.

It is the "thin blue line" of these officers that determines how democratic and fair the legal system is to all. Society cannot be at war with its law enforcement agents, be they police, sheriff's deputies, or officers within other law enforcement agencies. Nor should these officers determine what punishment should be delt to those that offend. Society should determine what is legal and what should be punished through the power of the individual vote and its elected representatives. Regrettably, some officers forget this.

With the increasing use of computer surveillance and artificial intelligence, the state's police power is more than ever becoming the Orwellian Big Brother. In this story, when the police abuse their power and then use the justice system to cover up a murder committed by one of their own, Drew Hawke steps up to right the wrong. In doing so, the young lawyer tries to use the same cyber power the police use to fight crime. But can Drew overcome the formidable power of the Blue Code of Silence police officers rely on to survive? His ability to break that code will determine whether he lives or dies.

While this story is fictional, its foundation regarding rogue law enforcement officers is not, as documented in numerous sources, including:

- Hearing on "deputy gangs" opens with testimony: Former LA undersheriff admits he had a deputy gang tattoo, *Los Angeles Times*, May 24, 2022
- LA sheriff deputy gangs "are a cancer," *Los Angeles Public Press*, March 8, 2024
- Hearings held into allegations of deputy gangs in LA County Sheriff's Department, LAist, May 31, 2024
- Video interview of Sheriff Alex Villanueva admitting existence of gangs, *LAist*, May 25, 2022.

# Cops Gone Bad

## An A. J. Hawke Legal Thriller

# CHAPTER ONE

**Twenty years ago**

Autumn weather gripped Southern California. A cold Alaskan current flowed south down the Pacific Coast. The accompanying cool marine air clashed with hot Santa Ana winds blowing west from the inland deserts. At sunset, a heavy mist hung along Pacific and Mission Beaches. As the evening progressed, the mist formed into a thick, moist fog covering the city of San Diego.

Flashing red lights painted the city's tall buildings as a San Diego police car followed a black BMW sports car. As the police cruiser closed in on the sports car, it sounded its siren, commanding the car ahead to pull over. Instead, the BMW accelerated west along Market Street, making a sharp left turn and almost colliding with parked cars as it sped south into San Diego's East Village.

A second police cruiser swept in from a side street, nearly clipping the BMW's rear bumper. The cruiser swerved to the left, its driver trying to turn south in pursuit of the fleeing car. However, its speed on the damp pavement was too much. The black-and-white scraped against a parked Toyota. The sound of metal grinding against metal and the tearing loose of the Toyota's driver's-side mirror, echoed off the surrounding structures. Undeterred, the chase continued south. From the damaged police car, a voice from its loudspeaker ordered the BMW to pull over.

The sports car made another abrupt left turn, heading east toward Interstate 5. A police helicopter joined the pursuit. It shined its spotlight on the fleeing car and ordered the BMW to stop.

"There is no exit," a voice from the Airbus H-125 chopper's loudspeaker announced over the roar of its whirling blades. Its bright light illuminated three police cruisers blocking the escape route to the freeway. The BMW's driver slammed on the brakes, which caused the vehicle to slide sideways on the wet pavement, slowly coming to a stop. The doors swung open and three dark-clothed youths ran from the vehicle.

The two pursuing police cars came to a halt; an officer exited from each vehicle and ran in pursuit of the suspects. In the distance, shots rang out, followed a few moments later by another single shot. Police from every corner of the East Village blocked the surrounding streets as groups of officers, guns drawn, ran in the direction of the gunfire.

Five minutes later, another police car rolled up and a young, newly striped San Diego Police sergeant exited the vehicle.

"Sergeant over here . . . over here," shouted an officer.

"Pat, what do we have? I heard over the radio 'shots fired.'"

"Yes, Sergeant. We have two suspects who are wounded. That guy being loaded into the ambulance fired at Tom. He fired back, hitting him and his buddy. I got to the scene a few minutes after. The other wounded perp, over there on the ground, he's in bad shape too."

At that moment the ambulance sped off, its siren blaring.

"What about the one in the ambulance?"

"The medics said he's got a bad wound to the chest."

At that moment a second ambulance arrived and medics lifted the other man onto a gurney.

"Where's the gun?" asked the sergeant.

"Tom has it," Pat replied, pointing to the officer in the middle of four other uniformed police officers.

"Where's the third guy?"

"I don't know, Sergeant. I lost him. Once I heard shots, I ran to the sound of gunfire to back up Tom. We're scouring the area now."

The sergeant pushed a mic button on his blouse. "Dispatch, connect me to the lieutenant."

"Yes, Sergeant."

A moment later a voice sounded through the shoulder microphone. "Sergeant, are you at the scene?"

"Yes, Lieutenant. Request permission to set up a second perimeter ten blocks from the current secured area. The third suspect is still at large and probably headed toward the community college area or even Balboa Park."

"Tony, you got the command of the things until I arrive," advised the lieutenant to his new sergeant. "Go ahead and secure as much area as you see fit. Just get the son-of-a-bitch."

"Yes, sir."

"Tony, I asked the CHP to dispatch two more units to help cover the area. They will call you once in position. I also dispatched a second chopper for the search. The H-125 had to refuel."

"Yes, sir."

The sergeant turned to the officer at his side. "Pat, I want you to set up the second perimeter. Make sure all units have the suspect's description. He is to be considered armed and dangerous."

"Yes, Sergeant."

"And, Pat, send two officers to the ER. I don't want either of those perps walking out."

"Understood, sir. Wouldn't look good if one of the suspects in your first officer-involved shooting escapes."

"Neither one is going anywhere," the sergeant said, smiling at his ex-partner's poor attempt at humor as he walked over to the group of officers. As he approached the five officers, he asked, "Tom, where's the gun?"

When none of the officers replied, he raised his voice. "Tom!"

"Here, Sergeant. Here's the perp's gun," came the belated reply as Tom handed the weapon to his sergeant.

"Tom, what are you doing? That thing should be in an evidence bag. Did you handle it without gloves."

"Yes."

"Why? You're contaminating evidence! You should know better."

"I had to take it from the guy's hand after I shot him."

"Bag it now. I want the pavement where you picked up the gun marked and photographed with the gun. And make sure you say how and why you touched the gun in your report. I want details."

The officer started to turn away when the sergeant called him back. Just then another patrol car pulled up, but the sergeant ignored it as he continued. "I know, Tom, you've been a police officer longer than me. But . . . it's *Sergeant* MacNeal, lest you forget."

"Yes, Sergeant. My lapse."

"Sergeant," shouted a lieutenant as he exited the newly arrived car.

The sergeant turned around and started to salute. "That's not necessary, Tony," the lieutenant said as he walked up. "Let's not forget we're in the East Village. Not exactly a police-friendly neighborhood. No telling what these long-haired wackos will do."

"Yes, sir."

"Now, what about this officer-involved shooting?"

"Two of our officers were in foot pursuit of the carjackers."

"Yes, yes, I was listening."

"When the suspects split up, Tom pursued the two running east. Pat went after the third, who ran north. Apparently, the pair at some point turned to face Tom. One of them shot at him. Tom returned fire, putting both down. EMTs just took them to the hospital. I assigned two officers to guard them."

"Good. Is Tom okay?"

"Yes, Lieutenant."

"And Pat?"

"Pat's okay, Lieutenant," responded the sergeant.

"Who witnessed the shooting?"

"No one. Tom was alone."

"I see, Sergeant, you have yellow tape up," the lieutenant said as he looked around. "Sounds like you've got it under control. I'll set up my command post over there. Tony, walk the scene with me."

As the two walked, the lieutenant said, "Sergeant, keep me appraised of the search for the third crook."

"Yes, sir."

The two stopped as the lieutenant surveyed the area of the shooting. "What's this?" he asked, pointing to several expended shell casings. "Mark those."

"Yes, sir. I haven't walked the area yet, sir. Sorry."

"Nothing to worry about. Just make sure the techs know where the perps were when shots were fired."

"Absolutely."

The lieutenant continued to look around as they walked until he saw another group of officers talking amongst themselves. "Sergeant, tell those officers with their thumbs up their asses to disperse all the looky-loos," he said, pointing to the gathering crowd. "Tell those idiots taking pictures it's all over unless they want us to confiscate their phones so we have a copy of the scene they're photographing. That should get them scurrying back into their holes."

"Yes, sir."

"By the way, Tony, good job all around. Send Tom over. I'll be at my car checking with dispatch."

# CHAPTER TWO

## Present day

Attorney Andrew J. Hawke, office manager Debbie McCaleb, college student and file clerk Matt Van Dryden, and a young associate attorney, Elizabeth Bernquist, sat in the law office conference room in the old George J. Keating Building. Being a Friday, they were going over the firm's calendar for the coming week when in walked a Hispanic man in a blue Ace parking shirt, baggy Dickie work pants, and black tennis shoes: Mario Rodriguez, the attendant for the Ace parking lot across the street from the Barleymash Café. Drew rose and walked out to greet his longtime friend.

"Hey, Mario, something wrong with my car?"

"No, me cuido mucho."

"Mario, English, please."

"The Beemer, she good. My friend Miguel not so good. I need to talk to you," said the distraught-looking attendant.

"Go into my office. I'll be right in," Drew said as he turned and opened the conference room door. "Debbie, I need to talk with Mario. Go ahead and finish up without me. Liz, as soon as Mario and I are done, we have to talk about the SMA Construct v. C.T.I. case. And, guys, I need to know who is handling what appearances next week."

When Drew entered his office, Mario stood looking out the large, third-floor window.

"What's up, Mario? You look as if you have the weight of the world on your shoulders."

"Sí. One of my good amigo's padre, he's been arrested. Es serio, muy serio," Mario added.

"Why was he arrested?"

"Murder . . ." Mario paused. ". . . because he stole a car years ago. He got a ten-year sentence. He served six long years before they let him out." Mario took a deep breath. "The *man* just won't leave him be. Now they arrest him again. I told my amigo Miguel and his mother you could help. You know, like you helped me after I got out."

"Sure, if I can. Tell me about the murder."

"It happened long ago. You gotta talk to Miguel."

"Miguel's the son?"

"Sí."

"Call Miguel and get him in here. What's his dad's last name?"

"Guerra."

"Got it. Call Miguel now. I need to see him this afternoon."

ooooo

It was nearly 1:30 p.m. when Miguel Guerra walked into the law office.

"Good morning, may I help you?" Debbie asked.

Miguel stood staring at the elderly black woman seated behind a desk. The late-twenty- something man appeared unsure of what he should say. Finally, he spoke.

"I'm Miguel Guerra."

"Yes, of course. One second, please." Debbie buzzed Drew's phone. "Miguel Guerra is here."

"Send him in."

Debbie rose and stepped to Drew's office door. She held it open as he walked past her. Drew stepped around his desk and introduced himself.

"Miguel, I'm Drew Hawke."

"I know. Mario said I could talk to you."

"Have a seat. Tell me what's wrong," Drew encouraged as he started to sit on the sofa next to Miguel's chair.

The young man, obviously nervous, started to rise but Drew just smiled. "It's okay. Relax. You can stay seated."

"Thank you . . . sir, ah . . . my father was just arrested for a murder that occurred nearly twenty years ago during an armed carjacking. But, Mr. Hawke, he didn't shoot the guy. A cop did."

"Why did the officer shoot the guy?"

"I don't know exactly. They were running from the police."

"Do you know why the police were chasing them?"

"Not exactly. But the cop said someone shot at him."

"I see."

"You gotta talk to my father. He can tell you. This all happened when I was a kid. Mom never said much about why dad was in prison. Please, sir, Mario said you're a good attorney. But we don't have any money. My mother and I don't know what to do."

"Miguel, don't worry about the money. I'll go and see your father. You don't have to pay me for such a visit. Afterward, I will decide if I can help your father. If not, you can get a free public defender."

"They're nothing but dump trucks. They made my father plead back then. That's why he went to prison."

"Okay. Tell your mom I will see your father this afternoon."

"Thank you, sir."

"What is your father's full name?"

"Carlos Guerra-Lopez. My name is Miguel Guerra-Dias. My mother's family name is Dias."

"I see. Do you know your father's date of birth?"

"Yes, Mario said you would want it. Here, Mr. Hawke, I wrote everything down for you." The man rose and extended his hand.

Drew took the note and shook Miguel's hand. "Great. I will see your father. Does he speak English?"

"Yes, of course."

"Call and tell him I will see him late today."

"Thank you, Mr. Hawke."

At 5:45 p.m. a black BMW pulled up next to the entrance of the San Diego County Jail. Drew Hawke backed the Beamer into a parking space designated "Official Vehicles Only." The young lawyer reached into the glove compartment and pulled out a placard which read in bold black ink, "San Diego County Sheriff's Department." The lawyer placed the placard on the dashboard, making sure the entire placard was visible so all three lines underneath the bold letters could be read, including the signature by the sheriff himself.

The lawyer entered through the visitor door and observed a boyish-faced deputy sheriff who sat behind a shield of bullet-proof glass. Deputy Burt Walls pushed the intercom button.

"Good evening, Mr. Hawke. Here to visit a client?"

"Evening, Burt. You got the desk duty again, I see."

"Yes, sir. Beats zoo duty."

"You know, Burt, we've known each other long enough to be on first names."

The young man smiled. "Indeed, sir. Who's your client?"

"Carlos Guerra-Lopez."

The deputy scanned the inmate list. "Yes, here he is. Another murder case, I see. Does this mean I'll see you on the news again?"

"I hope not. Too much publicity can be more of a problem than a blessing. Here's my bar card and driver's license," the attorney said as he pushed them through the slot under the glass shield.

Burt picked up his phone and called one of the cell blocks. "Jack, Deputy Walls, front desk. Is Guerra-Lopez available? His attorney is here to see him." After a pause, he continued. "Great." The deputy looked at Drew, nodded, and hung up the phone.

"You're in luck, Mr. Hawke. He just got back from dinner. I'm sure you know the procedure, but I'm supposed to tell visitors no matter who they are: A deputy will come through the door to your right and escort you upstairs. When you return, I will give you back your identifying documents."

"Thanks, Burt," came the reply as the lawyer turned and took a few steps toward the door, which bore a large sign:

**VISITORS: No weapons, guns, knives,**
**pepper sprays of any kind**
**or any sharp objects.**
**You will be searched.**

After a few minutes, the door opened and a tall, muscular deputy sheriff with a rather stern look to his countenance gestured for Drew to follow. He took the visitor to an elevator, which they rode to the fourth floor.

"Exit to your right, Counselor." The deputy followed and said, "Just a second, Counselor."

Drew stopped. The deputy stepped around the lawyer and

pulled open the door to a small room. The room was no more than ten feet by eight feet, with a glass partition separating the room from a similar room across from where Drew would sit. Drew was familiar with the routine, but this deputy seemed to be a rather by-the-book fellow, so Drew said nothing.

"You will meet inmate Guerra there," the deputy said, pointing to the room on the other side of the glass.

"When Guerra comes in, the two of you can talk over the phone to your right. Push the red button in front of you when done, and I will come and escort you downstairs."

"Thank you, Deputy," Drew replied.

Five minutes later another deputy opened the door to the room opposite and a Hispanic man in a red jail jumpsuit with deep furrowed lines across his forehead entered. Drew pointed to the phone to the man's left so the two could talk. They each picked up their respective telephone handsets.

"Please have a seat, Mr. Guerra-Lopez. I'm attorney Andrew J. Hawke. Your family asked me to come and see you."

Mr. Guerra-Lopez stood, looking at the young lawyer, then sat, holding the phone to his ear, but said nothing.

"Carlos, your son said you've been arrested for a murder which occurred during a car theft twenty years ago. That seems unfair, since you've already served time for the carjacking."

The man looked intently at Drew but still didn't speak.

*This routine I've seen before. Nobody in here trusts anybody else, especially a lawyer,* Drew thought.

"Mr. Guerra . . . may I call you by your father's last name, Guerra?"

Still no answer. "Mr. Guerra, anything we say to each other is confidential. It's protected by attorney-client privilege, which only you can waive. The sheriff cannot record what we say."

The man continued to look at Drew as if not believing what was said.

"Look, even if they did break the law and tape us, they couldn't use what we say." Still no response.

"Okay, I know you don't trust attorneys, especially a public defender. Miguel told me. But I am a private attorney and handle only serious felonies, which your case is."

Drew maintained eye contact. This was not the time to show a sign of weakness or undecidedness. It was obvious the man was deciding whether to talk, so Drew just waited.

Finally, the attorney spoke again. "Your son said he would call you and tell you I was coming to see you. I hope he told you I am here to help."

"You look very young for a lawyer," the fifty-year-old felon said.

"Yes, sir. But trust me, I know what I'm doing and I know how to win. From the limited information Miguel gave me, it seems there are several possible defenses I could raise on your behalf. If you are not interested, then I will not waste your time any further."

Drew waited a few seconds then spoke again. "Sorry to waste your time," he said and started to hang up.

"Have you ever won a criminal trial?" came the voice over the phone.

Drew lifted the phone back to his ear. "Yes, sir. All of them, and they were not traffic tickets. My last five trials were murder cases, which I won for my clients. If you talk to other inmates, they will know my name, A.J. Hawke."

The man seemed to relax somewhat given the attorney's confident manner.

"Mr. Guerra, I'm not here to sell you. I'm actually deciding whether you and your case are something I am interested in. To take your case, I need you to answer a few questions."

"How much do you charge?" came the reply.

"It all depends. If you answer my questions, I can tell you what I think of your case and whether I can help you. Let's start this way—why did you plead to an armed carjacking?"

"My public defender says he's got a deal and I should take it." Guerra paused, then added, "Otherwise I bite the Hot One."

"By 'Hot One' you mean go down for first-degree murder?"

"Yeah, what else?"

"Why were you being charged for murder?"

"The cop killed Juan."

"Go on."

"The government lawyer told me the law says I'm to blame for Juan's death 'cause I was part of the jack," Guerra said with an air of disgust in his voice.

"You mean the public defender?"

"Yeah."

"Go on."

"He said I had no defense. No lawyer could help me. Man . . ." he paused, shaking his head. "I was just a kid and a lawyer was telling me I had no choice. So I took the deal after he said I could get out in five to seven. Otherwise, I would never live long enough to get out or see my grandchildren."

"Were you at the scene when shots were fired?"

"No, but I heard them. I think I was about four blocks away at the time. Several hours later the cops cornered me and turned a dog loose."

"I see. After you got out of prison, what did you do?"

"I got a job and took care of my family. I've tried my best . . . provide, you know . . . be a good father . . . be a good husband.

The children are good kids. I rely a lot on Miguel. He works and helps to pay the bills."

"Any trouble with the police?"

"No way. It's 'yes, sir, no, sir.' I never piss the *man* off."

"Don't lie. I will find out everything once I pull your rap sheet."

"No way, man. I'm clean. I was just nineteen when my friends said come along. We're gonna have fun. I didn't know what was up until things got real hot. Manny pulled a gun and told this guy we needed a ride."

"What's Manny's last name?"

"De Jesus, Manny De Jesus."

"Was Manny the one that died?"

"No. It was his older brother, Juan."

"How do you know Juan De Jesus was killed by a cop?"

"Manny told me."

"When did Manny tell you how Juan died?"

"They sentenced Manny to life for shooting at a cop. After a couple of years, we both ended up at Pelican Bay."

"You were confined at the SHU?"

"Nah. We weren't in the 'hole.' We talked during rec."

"You mean you were part of the general prisoner population, and when they let you out in the yard to exercise, you two talked?"

"Yeah."

"And you were not in the Solitary Housing Unit?"

"No solitary."

"Okay. So what did Manny say happened. I need exact words, especially about the shooting."

"Can't give exact. Too many years. But what I remember is, they couldn't run no more. When they stopped, they both put their hands up. Manny's older brother said, "Don't shoot. We're unarmed." But the cop said you got to pay. Something about trashing a car. Then he shot both of them."

"Where was the gun . . . the one you guys used to steal the car?"

"I didn't steal nothing, man. There you go."

"My bad. I chose the wrong words. I meant who had the gun when the officer fired?"

"Manny told me he dumped the gun as they ran. Still, the bastard shot them anyway."

"You're saying the officer shot unarmed men?"

"That's exactly what Manny said."

Drew looked down. *Ah, man, this is a little hard to believe. A police officer shooting unarmed suspects. And all over a damaged car.*

Drew stared the man in the eyes and said, "Here are my rules, Mr. Guerra. You lie to me, I leave. I will not represent a liar. No fabricated stories. I work with the truth only. Trust me, the way you lose at trial . . ." Drew paused. ". . . is when you lie and get caught. You understand?"

"Mr. Hawke, that guy's a bad cop. Others in prison told me they knew the man . . . he was on the take. Probably still is."

Drew started to say something but the man placed the palm of his hand on the glass, as if to say "hear me out."

"Look, man. This was 'real talk,' con to con, private shit. I'm telling you what I know; what others told me. Prison is a very dangerous place. You don't go around making shit up, especially about cops being on the take. No one dares to tell lies. Guys get 'Molly Whopped' by a guard or some con . . . real bad. I mean real bad . . . like fractured skull, mutilated face, near-death stuff. What is said has a way of coming back

. . . even killing you. No, sir, I'm not making any of this up. He's just a bad man, Mr. Hawke. Real bad cop."

"Okay, Mr. Guerra. I'm interested in being your attorney. Do you want me?"

"Sure, why not. At least you're not a public defender. And Miguel did speak highly of you."

"I must say, Mr. Guerra, that is not exactly an enthusiastic yes, but it's a beginning. As of now I represent you. Do not talk to anyone about your case or what we talk about. That includes your family. The authorities can tape your conversations with them, even your phone calls to them. They can't when I talk to you. It's part of your constitutional rights. I will contact you in a couple of days. I'll give my card to a deputy who will pass it on to you. You can call collect if you want to talk to me at any time."

"But, Mr. Hawke, the money?"

"Right now I am representing you pro bono. You pay nothing. If things change later, we will talk. Now, I'm working for free. I will see you at your arraignment, where we will discuss how to get you out of here and home so you don't lose your job."

"Thank you, sir. Thank you."

# CHAPTER THREE

**Tuesday the following week**

Department 9 of the San Diego Superior Court was in the midst of the morning arraignment calendar.

"Call the next case, Madam Clerk."

"Yes, Your Honor."

"The State of California vs. Carlos Guerra-Lopez."

"Counsel, please state your appearances."

"Jack Farrat for the People," responded the tall, thin Assistant District Attorney.

"A.J. Hawke for Carlos Guerra-Lopez, who is appearing via video from the county jail."

"Mr. Hawke, your client is charged with murder in the first degree. How does he plead?"

"Not guilty to all charges, Your Honor."

"I take it, Mr. Hawke, your client is waiving formal reading of the charges in the complaint?"

"My apologies, Your Honor. Yes, sir. I have reviewed the complaint with him, and we have thoroughly discussed the allegations."

"Is that correct, Mr. Guerra Lopez?"

"Yes."

"Very well. Then let us proceed to set dates."

"If it pleases the court, my client does not waive time, and I request an immediate date for my motion to dismiss all charges."

"That is a rather unusual request, Mr. Hawke."

"I agree, Your Honor. But this is not your usual case. The murder was twenty years ago, and my client has already served time in jail for charges derived from the underlying offense. The very same case now charged in the complaint."

"Your Honor," petitioned the prosecutor as he rose.

"Yes, Mr. Farrat."

"Defendant Guerra-Lopez served six years for only the carjacking offense. The murder charges stem from a death that occurred during the car theft. Under the felony murder rule, he is absolutely guilty of murder since he pled to the underlying crime."

"I am well aware of my client's plea to carjacking, Your Honor. His plea goes to the heart of my motion. Since my client doesn't waive time, may I have the earliest date possible for my motion?"

"Mr. Farrat, I see no reason why Mr. Hawke can't have his early date. Do you object and if so, why?"

"Very well. The prosecution requests the normal briefing time for the motion."

"Mr. Hawke, when will you file your motion?"

"I could have it for you by the end of this week."

"Gentlemen, given the non-waiver of time, would one week from the date Mr. Hawke files his motion be enough time for the prosecution to file their opposition and one week thereafter for Mr. Hawke's reply?"

"Yes, Your Honor," Farrat replied. The judge looked to Hawke.

"Yes, sir," the young lawyer replied, "but I only need three days to write any rebuttal."

"Very well three days it shall be."

Drew persisted. "My client and I also request the court set a date for the preliminary hearing and for trial."

"Mr. Hawke, my calendar is crowded, if not unworkable."

Drew held his ground and waited. The jurist examined his calendar, then replied to Hawke's request.

"Here's what I'm going to do. Since you don't waive time, I will set your preliminary and trial dates after I hear your motion. If I understand what you are thinking, you may want to appeal any unfavorable ruling on your motion to dismiss. If that were the case, your appeal would automatically postpone trial. Am I wrong about your strategy?"

"Sir, Senate Bill 1437 changed the criteria for a conviction of an accomplice for felony murder. Not only does the bill establish a new standard for accomplice liability for felony crimes, but the bill specifically states it is retroactive, thereby establishing the criteria for any murder that occurred during a crime twenty years ago. My contention is that my client must be tried under the new felony murder standards."

"So you are adding that issue to your res judicata motion. Am I correct?"

"Yes. The two issues support one another."

"Your Honor."

"Yes. Mr. Farrat?"

"The language of 1437 concerns only those who were convicted under the old felony murder rule and are currently serving time."

"I believe, Mr. Hawke, 1437 could be construed as Mr. Farrat suggests. However, Mr. Hawke, your ideas are interesting. I look forward to reading both parties' briefs on the motion to dismiss. The preliminary hearing and trial dates will both be set after arguments on the defense motions."

"Thank you, sir. I don't wish to belabor this court with additional issues, but I need an expedited date for discovery."

"And what is that, Counselor?"

"Since we are not waiving time, I need the following. First, all police reports on the car theft and shooting of the De Jesus brothers, two of the theft suspects. In particular, I need the internal affairs shooting investigation notes and its final report. I know Mr. Farrat will object. But, sir, this is a twenty-year-old shooting and not many officers will be around. By my getting the internal affairs report, I can get to the bottom of this case and whether 1437 applies. I can't provide a defense for my client without such evidence."

"Mr. Farrat?"

"Obviously, I object to the release of any internal affairs reports or evidence."

"Why, Mr. Farrat? I doubt that there will be many witnesses to the shooting after such a long time. I'm inclined to grant the motion. Mr. Hawke may want to use such evidence at the preliminary hearing. Do you have any specific reason why I shouldn't grant the defense request?"

"No, sir, but this is such a rushed affair."

"I agree. Here's my order. You will provide to me, under seal, all evidence, all police reports, including the internal affairs, and any other relevant evidence with your stated oppositions three days after Mr. Hawke files his motions. I will rule what is not to be released to the defense. However, it is my intent, Mr. Farrat, to release all such information to Mr. Hawke. Depending on my ruling, all or none of such information will be admitted at trial. I believe . . ."

"But, Your Honor," injected Farrat.

"As I was about to add, Mr. Farrat, Mr. Hawke has a right to understand what happened that day, and if matters arise during trial he thinks merits reconsideration, he can then argue for the admission of any excluded material. Agreed, gentlemen?"

Both attorneys agreed.

"Yes, Mr. Hawke, there is more?"

"Sir, my apologies, but you haven't decided the issue of bail."

"Mr. Farrat, do your opposed bail?"

"Absolutely. The charge is murder in the first degree."

"Mr. Hawke, your position?"

"My client was a model prisoner. He has successfully completed parole. Equally important, he has led a crime-free life for nearly fourteen years, not even a traffic ticket. To detain Mr. Guerra in jail while all these legal matters are sorted out would be devastating to his family financially as well as emotionally. Mr. Guerra will lose his job if he sits in jail. His family lives on the income he earns from month to month. He is not a flight risk.

"Mr. Farrat."

"I don't know any one, Your Honor, who faces life in prison or the death penalty for first-degree murder that isn't a flight risk. That's why the courts grant no bail on first-degree murder charges."

"If I may respond."

"Of course, Mr. Hawke."

"Your Honor, at the root of everything we do in criminal law is the concept that society punishes a person for their crime, requires a prolonged period of supervision through parole, and, if successful, we say the offender has paid his debt to society. Mr. Guerra has done exactly that. He has earned our trust. To punish him further while he fights these charges is an unwarranted punishment to his family and him."

Farrat started to speak, but the judge raised his hand.

"Gentlemen, the court will decide the issue of bail at the preliminary hearing. Madam Clerk, note that the issue for bail is to be decided at that time."

The judge looked back at Drew. "I'm sure, Mr. Hawke, you agree that is the fairest way since the preliminary hearing will provide enough facts about the crime involved and Mr. Guerra's part in it for us to come to a proper decision."

The judge turned to his court clerk. "Madam, please note that I order the Probation Department to prepare recommendations for bail so I may have it at the preliminary hearing. Such a report is to be given to the district attorney, defense counsel, and the court no later than three days before the prelim."

"Ladies and gentlemen," the judge announced as he rose, "this court will now take a twenty-minute recess. Madam Clerk, please join me in my chambers and bring the calendar for the next three months."

Once outside of the courtroom, Farrat unleased a vicious tirade at Hawke. "What the hell are you doing? Your motion is ridiculous. There is no way a judge, or for that matter the Fourth District Court of Appeals, is going to let a defendant go just because he pled to a carjacking twenty years ago. The fact we are now prosecuting him for murder is irrelevant. A man died for God's sake."

"You know, Jack, you shouldn't moralize to me about a killing. What you are doing is a death sentence to Carlos Guerra and his family. So don't preach to me. The last thing you think about are those accused. What's important to you is how many convictions you can get and how long you can warehouse a person in prison."

"You're wrong, Hawke. These people are scum."

"A nineteen-year-old is not scum. Don't you realize putting

a youth in jail for six and a half years when he should be furthering his education and developing skills for his future scars him forever—literally relegating him to a life of near poverty?"

"So society is responsible for the immoral and deprived actions of these crooks. I think you have a fairytale conception about real life, Hawke."

"Not everyone comes from a privileged life of wealthy white parents like you," replied Drew.

"You should talk. You seem to have done quite well, Drew . . . even without a father, one that supposedly married your mother and then mysteriously died right after you were born."

"You shithead. How dare you call me a bastard."

"Those are your words not mine."

"If you weren't such a skinny-assed weasel, Farrat, I would beat the shit out of you right here."

"I think we are done, Hawke. Once again, you resort to your primal instincts, just like those young punks did twenty years ago."

With that, Deputy District Attorney Farrat walked off, leaving Drew not only furious but frustrated.

ooooo

Once Drew got back to the office, he gathered everyone in the conference room.

"Here's what's going on. Mr. Guerra says an officer shot the De Jesus brothers after they surrendered. Something about cop justice for hitting a car. At first blush, not very believable. But we gotta check it out. Could be a way to get him out of this mess. So, here's the plan. I informed the court I wished to file a motion to dismiss because the DA is pursuing a murder charge against our client as an accomplice for which our client already served time for the underlying car theft. The court said I could file it by the end of this week."

Debbie interrupted. "Drew, that's not much time."

"Yes, but necessary." Drew looked to Elizabeth. "Liz, have you been able to find any court rulings on Senate Bill 1437 being applied retroactively?"

"No. Not where the defendant is now being charged under the old accomplice standards as our DA has done."

"From my quick research over the weekend, that's exactly my conclusion. Good."

He turned to Matt. "I want you to go to the courthouse now and pull the original De Jesus and Guerra court files. Get everything, including the sentencing reports, which I hope includes all police reports. Those reports should tell us how the carjack and shooting went down. We need to know everything about the De Jesus-Guerra case."

Matt started to leave but Drew gestured for him to stay. "You need to know everything we're doing. I need you to help with other stuff.

"Liz, please prepare a special discovery motion for a court order to require the police and the County Probation Department to provide us with all reports on the De Jesus-Guerra carjacking. That includes the internal affairs investigation report on the shooting and the probation department's sentencing recommendations to the court. Let's not wait for them to object to producing internal investigation reports. We can't have discovery drawn out since we asked for an early trial date. Also, Liz, include a separate demand for the DA to provide all evidence supporting their decision to prosecute the murder twenty years later. The DA must have some new evidence."

Liz was writing furiously and nodding.

Drew continued. "Oh, the judge said the DA is to submit his discovery under seal if Farrat objects to anything."

"So the judge will decide if we get it," Liz asked as she hurriedly wrote to catch up.

"Correct."

When she looked up, Drew smiled. "Tell me if I'm going too fast."

"I'm ready."

"Now, second, I want you to analyze whether the old crime's facts support prosecution under the new standards for charging an accomplice with murder. You know what's required by Senate Bill 1437. What Matt gets from the courthouse records might contain the preliminary hearing record with transcribed witness testimony. If so, use those as our primary evidence of why Guerra should not be prosecuted under 1437's new standards for charging an accomplice for murder." Drew paused momentarily.

When Liz looked up, he began again. "And, third, research whether a Fifth Amendment double jeopardy motion can be argued. Under the old felony murder rule, a co-conspirator could be charged if the killing occurred during a felony carjacking. Guerra says he was originally charged with both murder and carjacking. We want to say since the intent to kill is implied from an armed car theft, he can't be charged for the murder now since he pled only to the car theft and was sentenced."

"Drew, I don't think the Fifth Amendment applies, since a defendant can be tried twice for the same criminal act as long as the legal elements for each crime are different. The elements for murder are completely different from the elements for carjacking."

Liz started to say more but Drew interrupted.

"Liz, you're right. Just entering a guilty plea to carjacking doesn't mean Guerra can't be charged with murder. But I want to see if anyone has challenged the implied Mens Rae of intent to kill based only on a felony carjack. If so, what was their argument and how did the court rule. Further, if Guerra's plea was unconditional, we need to know why the murder charge was dropped. Did the DA offer a plea deal? Did the judge go along or did the DA dismiss the homicide on his own for lack of evidence?"

"So, I have to see if murder was charged, and, if so, how and why it was dismissed."

"Yes, Liz."

"I'll start on this immediately."

"Matt, when you're at court, look to see if those nineteen-year-olds had any other arrests or convictions."

"Yes, Boss."

# CHAPTER FOUR

**The following day**

Deputy Sheriff Donovan approached the open door of the presiding judge's chambers and knocked.

"Yes."

"Your Honor, the mayor and police chief are here to see you."

"Send them in."

After a moment or two, San Diego City Mayor Sam Sandleson and Police Chief James Shaughnessy stood at Judge Brian O'Shea's chamber door.

"Come in, gentlemen. Why the unexpected visit?"

"Judge, may I shut the door?" asked the police chief as the mayor took one of the two chairs in front of the judge.

"Yes, of course."

Once both were seated the mayor began.

"Brian, we have a potential mess on our hands."

"We do? You mean *you* do."

"No, sir, *we* do. Morgan Mayfield, Chief Shaughnessy, you, and I."

"What is that, Sam?"

"Not to throw James under the bus, but he authorized the arrest of Carlos Guerra and the district attorney filed murder charges against the prior felon."

"Why is that a problem?"

"Hawke is Guerra's attorney."

"Sam, I still don't understand."

"Guerra was involved in an armed carjacking twenty years ago with two brothers. The brothers were shot during a police chase. One of whom died. Once Guerra got out of prison for the car theft, he's been saying the officer shot the brothers while they were unarmed. James allowed his detectives to arrest Guerra for murder based on the twenty-year-old accomplice's death."

"You mean under the felony murder rule?"

Yes. Now, A.J. Hawke is demanding all evidence relating to the carjacking and the shooting, including the department's Internal Investigation Division's findings, on the shooting."

"Judge, I had no alternative; my detectives demanded the guy be locked up," replied the police chief. "Now, Hawke is getting the internal investigation reports on the shootings."

"Guys, I still don't see the problem. Just because Drew Hawke is the defendant's attorney isn't something we haven't seen before."

"There are aspects about the shooting that shouldn't be made public."

"In other words, Jim, it was a questionable shoot."

"Yes, sir."

"I still don't see why we should be worried."

"Judge, the shootings occurred when Chief Shaughnessy was a lieutenant," spoke up the mayor. "A big stink about that investigation could cast doubts on my judgment for later appointing James as police chief. Voting is just a few months away on my re-election."

"Jim, how bad was the shooting?"

"I didn't shoot them, Judge. The now head of my detective division did. But the brotherhood of officers is standing with him. I can't go against my own officers. Besides, I had a big hand in internal affairs finding the shooting legit."

"I still don't see how all this affects us."

"The officer that did the shootings was an Enforcer."

"Jim, isn't that how those police officers handled street justice at the time?" asked the judge.

"Yes, sir. Fear through intimidation and worse. That was the rule of the day before I became police chief. But I've insisted this stop, and for the most part the rank and file have obeyed my order. Our problem," the chief added, "is that the officer who shot the kids knows what we've done."

"This isn't . . ."

"Yes, sir, Tom's the one."

"So you think our detective friend may try to do a deal with the district attorney if he is charged for the shooting."

"Judge, the two suspects were unarmed," added the chief.

"Brian, hasn't the statute of limitations run out," asked the mayor. "The shootings were twenty . . ."

The chief interrupted. "Sam, there is no statute of limitations for murder."

"I know, James. I know," Judge O'Shea confirmed, thinking he was being addressed. Still in deep thought, O'Shea raised his hand when the mayor started to speak.

"The problem is that damn district attorney won't play along on anything," the judge finally said. "Because of the case's age, he could handout a sweet plea bargain . . . say, no prison time for a plea. I'd make sure one of my judges went along. But oh, no, not that shithead. Every time I talk to him, he tells me, 'Brian, I'm an independently elected county official. I'll prosecute what I want. I don't need your advice.' He's just not a team player."

"J.R. Sutherland is a problem," confirmed the mayor. "I think he wants to be governor. We can't afford to have both

Hawke and the district attorney investigating that old shooting. They just might uncover what the Enforcers have done."

"What in the world possessed you, Jim? Why arrest the fool to begin with? The murder is too old to fiddle with."

"Judge—" replied the chief.

The judge waved his hand. O'Shea pulled open a drawer and switched on a device to prevent any outside surveillance recordings.

"Gentlemen, we should be having this conversation in the Sanctum."

"But, Judge, we have to decide what to do now," pleaded the mayor.

"Okay, but talk very low."

"Judge, like I started to say," persisted Chief Shaughnessy, "the real problem is that the Enforcers are still active. Any investigation into the shooting may uncover them. Tom is one."

"Why in the hell haven't you done something about them, Jim?"

"Judge, there are just too many of them. I've made myself clear. Things . . . things can't be done the old way. And, for the most part, the brotherhood is complying."

"You're right," said the judge. "If Southerland finds out the Enforcers still exist, he will ride this thing to either the state attorney general's office or the governor. He's a body climber. He doesn't care who he screws."

"Judge," asked the worried mayor, "what do we do?"

"Prison is a dangerous place," the judge murmured. "But still, Jim, why take the risk?"

"I guess the guys figured with Guerra in prison, he might shut up or even get killed like the other guy."

"The other guy!"

"The other one who got shot. He went down for his brother's murder and got shanked while in prison."

"For running off at the mouth, I assume."

"Don't know, Judge. All this happened before I became chief."

The judge slowly lifted his six-foot-five, two-hundred and forty-pound body out of his chair and walked around the room. Chief Shaughnessy stiffened when the hulking frame of the man stopped behind him.

"Jim," O'Shea said, placing both hands on the chief's shoulders, "I want you to take care of this fuck-up. As I see it, Sam may have no option but to fire you if your part in this comes out."

"But, Judge, I've made reforms."

"Jim, with you helping cover up the shootings and any suggestion that you know the Enforcers still exist, no one will believe you've done anything."

Walking back around his desk, O'Shea added, "Guys, you have to keep the Enforcers out of this. Sam, figure out a way to make this twenty-year-old case look like a waste of time. If you can, it will make that damn DA look like a fool for now prosecuting that guy. Gripe about the city's burgeoning crime problem. Ask why are we wasting manpower and resources on such an old case. Especially one where this guy already served time."

"Brian, that's putting me out on a limb. I'm supposed to be the law-and-order mayor. I'm Jim's boss. Criticizing the DA, or even the chief, makes me look like I don't know what I'm doing."

"Walk the line, Sam. Walk the line," Judge O'Shea said.

After a few moments of silence, with the mayor looking

at the chief for help, the judge smiled and added, "I've got it, Sam. Frame the issue this way: Crime is a growing problem. Demand that law enforcement agencies crack down on crime in our city. State you have ordered an increase in neighborhood policing. Hell, man, make it a public safety thing."

"That's good, Brian. I could say I've ordered the chief to reassign officers to high-crime areas and . . ."

"Be smart about it, Sam. You and your political hack, that Bodsly guy, figure out how to word it."

"You mean William Bodsly, my Deputy Chief for Innovation and Policy?"

"Call him what you want, Sam. We both know he's your political advisor. Ha . . . a political advisor on the city payroll. Sometimes, Sam, you walk the line too far."

"But judge . . ."

"Don't fret, Sam. I like your ingenuity. Back to business. Get Bodsly to come up with a new law-and-order plan."

"I see where you're going, Brian. By my saying I'm making a bold reorganization of policing, I put pressure on the DA to quit wasting resources on this old case."

"Be direct without referring to the Guerra matter. Sam, invite J.R. Sutherland to join you in your campaign to clear the streets of crime. In your news conference, say you intend to discuss with the DA about redirecting prosecution resources to gangs and current crimes. When you meet with Sutherland, casually ask if he can clear any old matters and lower-level cases off his calendar in order to have some of his lawyers join your new crime task force. Don't be obvious. Make it a casual part of your discussion on how he can use his resources to aid the new police effort. Invite him to make suggestions, yada, yada. Bodsly knows what to say."

"Judge, I like this. By having a couple of deputy DA's

attached to a countywide task force, we could shorten times for search and arrest warrants and make sure all arrests are clean," added Chief Shaughnessy.

"And, I can invite all the church, minority leaders, and anti-poverty groups to meet with me to see how they might help lower crime," stated Mayor Sandleson.

"Good ideas, guys. Sam, have the police chief with you when you make this announcement. Say the two of you intend to meet with all such groups."

"Brian, I think this might work. It will look good on the news," replied Mayor Sandleson.

"Okay, guys, we have a plan. Now, Sam, you, Jim, and Bodsly make it work."

All but Shaughnessy rose to leave.

"Judge, you got a minute?" the chief of police asked.

"Sure. There's more?"

"Brian, I'm not sure the old guard will go along with any deal that lets Guerra stay out of prison. What I'm hearing is they want him silenced, permanently."

"Jim, get those rogue dogs in line. Now. Tell them the mayor has an election to win. Hell, I could give a damn what they do to Guerra after the November election."

"I understand, Boss. But to these guys it's personal. It's their butt that could end up behind bars."

"Bullshit. I could give a damn. They created this mess, not us."

The police chief stood there wide-eyed and stunned. "Boss, the Enforcers are countywide, not just in my police department. I've got great influence, but not that much."

"Look, Jim, it's all about us controlling things. Control gives us power to do what we want. We need Sam as mayor of this city. He influences the city council and helps ram through Mayfield's real estate projects. Those projects line our pockets with money, including yours. So, if you want to keep your job, get everyone with the program. That includes those assholes who think only about themselves. You hear me?"

"Yes, sir."

# CHAPTER FIVE

## Friday evening

A spotlight panned the sky to the west announcing something special was about to happen. A white van proceeded east down Aero Drive and entered the palm-tree lined circular driveway leading to a three-story building behind the slow-moving light.

Two parking attendants ran up to the van as it came to a stop in front of the entrance to the Sheraton Four Points Hotel.

The short ride from San Diego's Gaslamp Quarter had been a quiet one. The driver, Warren Sullivan, hadn't said a word to anyone, especially to the main attraction of the night's event seated next to him. Even the normally loquacious Matt and his college buddy, Tyler, had been silent. The two college students scanned the brightly illuminated hotel and the lines of cars trying to get into the affair. The two 19-year-olds had never attended such a violent event.

The van's front passenger door opened and a tall, muscular-looking young man dressed in gray sweat pants and a hoody stepped out. One of the attendants looked at the man's hands, which were wrapped in white tape, and asked, "Here to fight?"

"Yes," came a confident response.

"Straight through the double doors to the hotel registration desk. They will sign you into your room, which will be on the main floor. The room will be next to the large conference hall. That's where the fights will be."

The tall man went through the double entrance doors and into the lobby hallway. He paused. At the end of the long hallway was a glass wall. Outside the glass was a large patio packed with well-dressed attendees engaged in what appeared to be lively conversations, apparently about the night's cage fights. Waiters walked amongst the crowd offering drinks. All seemed to be having a great time. The fighter turned and walked toward a smiling young lady dressed in a blue uniform standing behind the front desk.

"A.J. Hawke. I'm here for tonight's MMA event. The room may be under just Drew Hawke."

The woman checked the list of fighters and nodded. "Oh, yes, here you are Mr. Hawke."

The young woman looked up at the handsome man standing in front of her and added, "Nice to see you again, Mr. Hawke."

"Nice to see you again, Alex. Are you still studying at San Diego State?"

"I graduate this spring. I'm really excited," Alexandra said, seemingly totally distracted from what she was doing. "Oh, sorry. This is your card key. It's room 110."

Without taking her eyes off the well-built fighter, she smiled in an admiring way while she gave directions to the young but impressive man standing in front of her.

"Will you be watching the fights?" asked Drew.

"Oh, no. I have to work tonight."

"Well, if you can get away, I'm the fourth fight. Love to see you there."

The woman blushed. "I'm afraid fights are a bit too violent for me. But I wish you good luck."

Before Drew could flirt further, Warren and Drew's two-man entourage arrived with the fight gear and ushered the fighter off to Room 110.

Once in the room, Drew asked, "Warren, what's the hurry? We got over two hours before I fight."

"Look, Casanova, we got a lot to go over. You haven't even broken a sweat yet," came the reply.

"Hey, I'm ready. I was just being nice to her."

Before the distracting banter could go further, Matt interrupted. "Drew, here's your gear," calling attention to fighter's shoes, groin belt, compression shorts, and other items in the bag he was holding.

Warren took the gear bag and set it on a table. Matt then pointed to the face salve, grease, cut sticks, and smelling salts, asking further, "Where do you want me to put this stuff?"

"Leave them in the cut bag. We'll take them out to the cage when we're called. And keep the lid on the ice chest so the water bottles stay cold. I want you to fill the neck ice bag once we're out there."

Not missing a beat, Warren scanned the room. There in the corner on two large metal stands were the speed bag and large body bag he had requested. "Tyler, bring me the Twins' MMA black-and-red gloves," he commanded.

Warren grabbed each hand. He told Drew, "Make a fist. Hold them tight. Now relax them." He checked the wraps closely. They were still tight. He did a final tight wrap with some tape he pulled out of his pocket. He then slipped the gloves onto Drew's hands, one at a time, and laced them up. "How do they feel, champ?"

Drew closed each fist and punched the gloves together, striking the face of the gloves against one other. "They're great. Love Twins."

"All right, warm up on the bags. Slowly and lightly at first. Let the hands get seated into the gloves. Don't need any broken bones. You've got several hundred people out there who have paid to see San Diego's own fighting lawyer. 'The man who took down the Sphynx rapist.'"

"Very funny, Warren. Whose idea was it to make this such a publicity deal anyway?"

"I think it was Channel 12 that coined the phrase and started the PR rolling."

"I told you, Warren, I wanted it stopped. What happened?"

"By the time I contacted the channel, the other news outlets had picked it up."

"Damn, Warren, what am I going to do if I lose?"

"Just don't lose. Look, this Luke D'Angelo kid, he's really good. He's only twenty-five years old and has been training under his jiujitsu masters since fourteen. Like I said before, when we trained, he's a good grappler. Wants to get on his back and bring you in. So stay off the mat. He's slightly taller than you but lean, really lean and strong."

"Yeah, I know. I'm not as young and strong as I used to be."

"That's not the point. Luke's strong point is jiujitsu. He's a second-degree black belt and has great submission moves. Remember, this young police officer is the chief instructor in hand-to-hand combat at the police academy, which is why you've got to stay off the mat. Avoid his strengths," demanded the older fighter as he squeezed Drew's shoulders, making sure Drew was onboard with the strategy.

"Now look it, Drew, box him. Jab the shit out of him. Keep

going to your left. He's another lefty. By moving left, you keep his strong left punch further away. You've got great kicks so use them, but wait until he's really hurt before you try to put him away. Got it?"

"Yeah, yeah," said the lawyer, obviously having heard all this before.

"I agree, Warren, we've talked about this. I even went on my own and watched him fight at the El Cajon gym. He's not a bad boxer. He's especially effective with his long jab and follows them up with punishing lefts."

"All the more why you have to keep moving left. You're a better boxer and a harder puncher. Just stay in the middle of the cage and pound on him. If you hit him good, don't let him feint injury and sucker you in. He'll take you right to the mat. Luke executes the fastest Triangle choke holds in Southern California. The best defense is not getting caught in one when he tries to draw you close."

Drew nodded, knowing his longtime friend's advice was right on. Warren was a veteran cage fighter, and he'd trained Drew hard for this fight. The young man felt really good. Confident, but thanks to Warren's constant nagging, not cocky. Drew shed his sweats and began his routine on the speed bag.

"Remember, Drew," Warren yelled above the rhythmic sound of the bag, "D'Angelo is the best fighter we've faced. He's won all his fights to date. And by submission holds."

Drew nodded, thoroughly serious.

The first two fights before Drew's went all three rounds, giving Drew plenty of time to stretch, work the bags, and skip rope. He was sweaty and ready. But kept repeating the routine, first on the speed bag, then the big body bag, alternating back and forth between long sparing sessions with Warren.

Matt and Tyler sat and watched wide-eyed and yet fearful for their good friend who was about to be locked in a cage with an equally talented fighter.

A knock came at the door. Warren answered.

"You're up," came the command. "Follow me to the waiting area."

The four left the room. Drew was wrapped in a colorful silk robe, gray hoody, and a towel around his neck, all to keep the heat in and him loose.

Luke D'Angelo was first to enter the hall, following his jiujitsu master, with six MMA fighters from his club surrounding him. A strong crowd of police officers rose and cheered on their man.

Warren held up his hand. "Wait," he ordered. As D'Angelo unrobed Warren declared, "Now!" Drew followed head down with both hands on Warren's shoulders. Matt and Tyler completed the small entourage as they carried the gear. As soon as Drew entered, the crowd stood and a roar went up, "Hawke, Hawke, Hawke."

Drew was stunned but managed a smile in recognition. At the cage, the fighting lawyer unrobed. The referee checked each fighter, running his hands through their hair and around their ears. He checked their shoe soles and then their waistbands. The ref then tapped on their groin guards.

Satisfied each fighter was legal, the referee gestured toward the cage. D'Angelo entered first. Another roar went up from the group of fellow officers in attendance.

When Drew stepped in, a louder roar engulfed the room. The referee raised his hands for quiet and called the two fighters to the center of the cage. There he reviewed the rules of combat one more time. He then sent them to their corners and ordered the cage door locked. With a loud voice he yelled, "Get it on."

Both fighters approached, Drew circling to the left as planned. Neither struck out. Finally, Drew stepped to the left and forward, striking out with a jab and then a second and third. Each time D'Angelo blocked the punch or stepped to his left and away. Drew feinted to his right and quickly stepped to his left as D'Angelo threw a wasted left punch. Drew stepped in and landed a left jab, followed by a solid right. The police officer stepped back and shook his head, obviously feeling the blows from his hard-punching opponent. A roar went up as Drew stepped to his left again and followed up with two aggressive lefts and another solid right. The 25-year-old moved to the center of the cage. Drew followed, circling to the left.

Suddenly, the lawyer stopped and faced his opponent as the young man came closer. Drew snapped a hard right kick to the back of D'Angelo's left calf. The knee buckled. The two circled again only to have Drew snap another kick, buckling the leg, this time nearly forcing the knee to the canvas. D'Angelo stepped back and seemed to gain his composure. Drew circled to the right and went back to the left as the man threw a right jab, followed by a leaping left as Drew stepped out of range, leaving the fighter in an awkward position. Drew charged at his unbalanced opponent with a flurry of lefts and rights, driving D'Angelo back into the ropes. The man lingered on the ropes. Drew stepped back to the center of the cage.

The two continued to circle, looking for an opening. Both fighters seemed oblivious to the roars of the crowd. Suddenly, D'Angelo charged, grabbing Drew's thighs and driving him back into the ropes. Standing against the ropes, Drew slammed two hard rights, followed by a left to the sides of his opponent's head. But to no avail.

Hawke heard a voice from his corner above the yells of the excited audience. "Don't let him take you down."

But the strong man lifted Drew up in a move to throw the lawyer to the canvas. Drew immediately reacted by using his opponent's own strength and motion toward the canvas by twisting hard to the right, slamming both to the cage floor. Drew used his strength and forced himself on top of his attacker. Drew broke Luke D'Angelo's grip by slamming a left forearm into the side of his opponent's throat, followed by a head butt and a hard right to the face. To everyone's amazement, Drew maneuvered off of D'Angelo into a crouching position as D'Angelo rolled into a defensive guard position with his back on the canvas. But the lawyer didn't take the bait. Instead, he stood and stepped back, motioning for the fighter to get up and box.

As the younger man rose, blood trickled from his nose. Drew stepped back further, allowing him room to fight. D'Angelo cautiously moved toward Drew. The crowd was a buzz about what just happened. Voices could be heard asking why Drew hadn't followed up with fight-ending blows. The two circled again. As D'Angelo moved, a slight hitch to his movement became visible.

*Looks like my kicks are taking effect,* the lawyer said to himself as he looked for another chance to strike the injured leg, only to have the round end. Drew put both gloves out in a show of sportsmanship. D'Angelo did the same. The two turned and went to their corners.

Drew stood in his corner watching as the jiujitsu master talked to his charge, gesturing with his hands. Warren leaned over the ring ropes and whispered, "He's going to circle to his right to cut off your movement to the left. When your shoulders square to him, he will try either a left leg-sweep or a leading left followed by a takedown, so leave enough room to maneuver. Try to stay close to the center of the cage. Don't get cornered."

The bell rang and the two charged to the center, with Drew moving to the left. As Warren had warned, the fighter stepped right throwing a jab but missed as Drew took a half step to his right. To the fighter's surprise, Drew snapped another quick kick to the damaged left leg. This time Drew was off balance and it didn't land forcibly. But the psychological effect was obvious as the man stepped further to his right, followed by a hurried leg-sweep to Drew's legs. Drew simply stepped back, avoiding the sweep, and toward the off-balanced fighter, throwing a strong right kick to the left side of D'Angelo's head. The fighter staggered to his right two steps and went down to his knees, hesitated, and then bent his head down onto the canvas.

Drew charged the slumped body and started pounding on the sides of the man's face. Still stunned, the frenzied attack drew no response from the wounded fighter. As the referee moved closer, Drew threw five more punishing combinations. The 25-year-old, face down, didn't move to protect himself. The referee jumped in, grabbing Drew around the upper arms and yelling, "It's over. It's over. You won."

Drew stepped back as the referee knelt to check the fighter.

The bell rang loudly in a volley of clangs, followed by the fight announcer proclaiming, "It's over. It's over. Another Hawke knockout."

Those words could barely be heard over the roar of the crowd. The fight was indeed over as D'Angelo's corner rushed into the cage, followed by a doctor. Drew stood looking at the man still down as they rolled him first onto his back and then to his right side so he could breathe and not swallow his tongue. Warren rushed in, grabbing his fighter around the waist and lifting him off the ground, spinning the sweaty man around for all to see. Once A.J. came back to earth, Warren raised Drew's right arm high above his head as Matt jumped his idol, causing the tired man to take two steps back as the exuberant kid wrapped his legs and arms round his winner in a crushing bear hug.

Tyler followed, jumping up and down in joy and yelling, "What a fight. What a pounding. What a fight!"

Drew slowly put Matt down and raised a glove to his lips as if to say to Tyler that's enough. D'Angelo had regained his feet with the support of two of his MMA fighters. Drew walked over and whispered in the defeated fighter's ear, "Good fight. It could have gone either way. I got a lucky kick in."

The young man looked at Drew and embraced him. Drew said a few more words of praise to the man and the grateful fighter hugged him again.

"I'm okay. But you tagged me good." Then he added, "Hawke, your words are kind. You're a good man."

Drew placed a glove on the man's head, touching his forehead against D'Angelo's forehead. "Don't forget, I was just lucky."

The victorious fighter turned and started to walk back toward his corner to the adulation of the crowd but stopped. He turned to his opponent's jiujitsu master. Hawke clasped his gloves together and bowed in a traditional sign of respect. To Drew's surprise, the old master bowed his head in return, acknowledging the well-deserved victory.

The Hawke entourage moved to the cage door only to be met by a flurry of cell phone flashes and reporters yelling questions. Warren tried to make his way through the crowd, but it was just impossible. Drew stopped, raising his still-gloved hands so he could speak. "Thank you, folks. Look, Luke D'Angelo is a tough young man trained by a masterful sensei. He could have put me into a submission hold at any moment."

Someone in the crowd shouted, "Was your strategy to out box him?"

"Luke is an expertly trained jujitsu fighter. He almost had me on the mat at one point. I had to stay in the center of the ring and fight."

A TV reporter yelled, "Is this how you fought the Sphynx rapist?"

Drew smiled. "That was a completely different type of a fight. There was no referee to stop it. It was a fight to the end. Fortunately, the Sphynx's girlfriend, Silvia Estrada, didn't shoot me." The crowd laughed.

Drew again gestured and every one quieted. "Guys, I'm a little tired and need to take a shower. If you don't mind, how about we talk later."

The gathered throng stepped aside and started to clap in appreciation of the gracious and accommodating fighter.

# CHAPTER FIVE

**Saturday morning**

The sun shone brightly through the loft's tall windows as a man, half awake, with the covers kicked back, stared at the ceiling. He just lay there going over and over every step, feint, punch, and kick of the fight—his mind still consumed by the menacing, if not life endangering, fight of the previous night. Luke D'Angelo was not just a man he could lose to. The man was a jiujitsu black belt quite capable of doing more than choking someone into submission.

*Yeah, I was indeed lucky,* he thought. *D'Angelo was an expert in a martial art I am not.* Deep down inside Drew knew he should have lost to a better, more well-rounded fighter. The words of his old Thai master kept repeating in his mind, "Any man can kill you. Just don't give him the chance."

*Warren was right. I took the fight too lightly. I really didn't understand who D'Angelo was and how well he was trained.* A smile came over his face. *Neither did he know me. That's why he lost. He was just bothered too much by my kicks to the lower leg. Next time he will know what to do.* The thought sent a chill through his body. There is no more intense sensation than facing a beating or even death at the hands of another man. Drew Hawke lay there a moment longer, fully awake.

"Tami."

"Yes, Drew," answered the computer program.

"What time is it?"

"It is Saturday, 8:43 a.m. The weather will be warm and sunny. Are you ready to get up?"

"Yes, Mother Terresa."

"My name is Tami, not Mother Terresa. Are you making humor?"

"Yes, Tami."

"I will make a note. Mother Terresa is funny."

"Tami, no. It's just an expression. She is not funny or humorous or anything like that."

"Dully noted, Drew."

"Should I turn on the Keurig so the water is hot?"

"Yes, thank you."

"Very well. Keurig on."

Drew got up and went to the bathroom. When he finished, the man was still preoccupied with the fight. He felt his stomach. *I'd better do my crunches.*

Drew walked over to the chin-up bar in the corner of the large loft. He bent down and attached an inversion boot to each leg. He jumped up, grabbing the horizontal bar. Slowly, he lifted his legs up until he could hook the boots to the bar. The abdominis and oblique muscles tightened as he lowered himself until he was fully inverted. After a few deep breaths Drew began doing his daily one hundred inverted stomach crunches.

After what seemed an eternity, he finally counted out loud, "Ninety-seven, ninety-eight, ninety-nine, . . . oof . . . one hundred." There the lawyer hung upside down, taking deep rapid breaths, the four layers of horizonal muscles taut across his abdomen. His entire body glistened with sweat.

Finally, he looked toward the kitchen sink. "Tami, is the Keurig ready?"

"Yes, Drew."

Haltingly, he lifted himself up and grabbed the horizontal bar. Carefully, he elevated his legs until the inversion boots' hooks were above the bar. He lowered his legs, grimacing as his worn-out muscles complained until he was hanging vertically upright. The tired man then let go, landing on his feet. Drew rested bent over with his hands on both knees, breathing deep, slow breaths.

With the boots still on, Drew slowly walked to the counter. There he rotated the coffee rack until he found his favorite Jamaican dark-roasted K-cup. He inserted it, closed the machine's lid, and pushed the brew button. He opened the cabinet above the sink. He chose a large coffee mug. The hungry man looked through the cabinets, but as usual they were bare, except for a few Bobo's soft-baked peanut butter and jam-filled oat cookies. *They'll have to do.*

Drew poured the dark brew into the mug and downed two of the cookies while he sipped on his coffee. Still sipping his coffee, Drew walked over to the full-length mirror to check out how much damage D'Angelo had inflicted on his bod. Noting a few welts on his head, his sweaty bod appeared remarkably okay. *Yup, it could have been much worse. I was indeed lucky.* He took the boots off, took a few more last sips of his coffee, and headed to the shower.

Ten minutes later he emerged, wrapping himself in an extra-large towel.

"Tami, any phone calls or messages?"

"No, Drew. But someone was at the loft door early this morning. Shall I play back the video? They did not use the loft's intercom or ask to enter."

"Who was it?"

"Unknown. He did not identify himself."

"Yes, please turn on the video." Drew walked over to the armoire he had bought from an antique store and opened its doors. He stood there for a moment before he bent down and picked out of the dirty clothes basket a pair of gray sweatpants.

Back at the computer, Drew hit the play button. Sure enough, there was a man. But his face was shrouded by a hoody. Drew zoomed in but couldn't see the face as the man kept his head too covered. At the loft landing, the man pulled back the elevator safety gate. He bent down with something in his hand and then closed the gate. Drew immediately looked to the loft door. Something had been shoved under the door.

"Tami, freeze the video." Drew walked over to the door. It was a folded piece of paper. He opened it. His expression turned serious as he read the hand-scribbled note.

"Tami, text Pat De Luca immediately. Use the urgent emoji," Drew ordered as he began walking back and forth with the poorly written warning in his hand. The phone rang.

"Speaker phone, Tami."

"Speaker on."

"Hello, Pat?"

"Yes. What's the urgency. Did you get hurt last night?"

"No. Do you know what the 'Enforcers' are?"

"Did you say Enforcers?"

"Yes."

"How do you know about them?"

"Some guy slipped a note under my door."

"What's it say?"

"God, Pat you sound concerned."

"What's the note say!"

Drew read from the note: "the enforcers are coming after

De Luca. You shouldn't have taken the case. You're a good man, I had to tell you."

"Is the note signed?"

"No, Pat. Who are the Enforcers?"

"Drew, I'm on my way over."

"Okay. Pat, be careful." The phone clicked dead.

Twenty minutes later the elevator intercom buzzed. Drew looked at the computer screen.

"Come on up, Pat."

The slow-moving elevator finally jarred to a stop and De Luca stepped through the loft door held open by Drew.

"Where's the note?" commanded the old friend.

Drew handed him the piece of paper. Pat looked at the note intently. Finally, he spoke. "Let's talk." The two walked over to the sofa next to the computer and sat.

"Pat, is the note serious? You appear upset."

"Look, son, it's time we had a long talk."

The posture of the man and the tension in his voice had Drew fearing what was about to be said.

Pat began. "When I was a San Diego police officer, there existed a group of officers who took justice into their own hands. The group called themselves the Enforcers. They were frustrated with the legal system and the fact police officers risked their lives to arrest crooks only to see them released on technicalities or just get a slap on the wrist. These officers were so fed up they threatened petty crooks at the point of a gun for information or just brutally beat them as a warning. Others they paid to plant evidence, all in an effort to put away suspects they didn't have enough evidence to convict. Then there were those they just eliminated."

"O-o-h, Pat, were you one of those Enforcers?"

"*No!* But that's one of the reasons I left the force. They kept trying to involve me in their shit. You can only know so much without becoming a part of the illegal activity. If you stay quiet, you are conspiring to cover up the illegal acts. If you report them, you are a Judas amongst the blue brotherhood. So . . . I left."

"How come I or others haven't heard about the Enforcers before?"

"It's all protected by the blue wall of silence."

Drew nodded. "The unspoken code amongst officers not to report a colleague's errors, misconduct, or crimes."

"Yes, Drew. If you break the code, you pay a very harsh punishment, the worst being your fellow officers not coming to your aid when you call for help. A literal death sentence out in the field."

"So you got out while you could?"

"Yes. I turned in my badge. I was already thinking about leaving. Lauren and I wanted to help raise you. Your mom couldn't do it on her own, especially when you were a teenager."

"That's why you took me to Pop Warner, Little League, and later to the pool for water polo."

"Your mother wanted to do it all. She loved seeing you grow into a man. But between her court duties during the day, transcribing her court reporter shorthand notes at night, and helping you do the things a young boy should do, it was just too much for her. She was constantly sick as she wore herself down for lack of sleep and worry over not being there for you. So, Lauren, I, and of course Debbie, stepped forward."

"Oh, my God. I was the cause of mom's cancer."

"Don't you dare blame yourself. Cancer can strike at any time and to the healthiest of people. No, Drew. Lauren and I had no children so we thoroughly enjoyed helping. And

Debbie, you would think she was your mother by the way she hovered over you as a child. Sometimes too much."

Drew laughed. "She still does."

"We all did and your mother loved us for it. Remember, parenting is a father-and-mother job. With your father gone, we happily stepped in."

"I don't know what I would have done after she died. You guys were my only family left."

Drew was near tears when Pat brought things back to the present. "Drew, I'm going to send Lauren to live with her sister in Colorado."

"Why?"

"To get her out of danger."

"The note is about Guerra, isn't it? That's why it said they were coming after you?"

"Yes."

Drew wanted to know why they were threatening him but Pat just changed the subject.

"Let me look into this. Drew, the Enforcers have been silent for years. There's got to be a reason for this note. Let's talk later."

ooooo

A black BMW with its top up sat in the Third Avenue Ace parking lot diagonally across from the Chula Vista gym where Luke D'Angelo trained. Drew checked his watch: 2:00 p.m. Time for Luke's post-fight Sunday meeting with his sensei.

Twenty more minutes passed. Drew was beginning to think the guy on the gym phone was wrong. Suddenly, the door to the gym swung open. D'Angelo and two other men stepped out and stopped.

*What are they talking about. D'Angelo pointing to the right side of his jaw. That's where my match-ending kick landed.*

One guy wrapped his arms around Luke and the three exchanged fist tapes. Luke turned and walked with a slight limp across Third toward the parking lot where Hawke had parked. Drew opened the driver's door and stepped out.

"Luke," Hawke called out.

D'Angelo looked and stopped. "What are you doing here," he asked as Drew walked toward him.

"Thanks for the note under my door."

The young officer looked around. "Shush. What are you doing? You shouldn't be here."

"Sorry, but your note didn't say why De Luca was in danger. Did I do something wrong?" asked Drew.

"Damn it, Hawke, you're going to get me in really bad trouble," replied D'Angelo as he kept walking to his car.

"Luke, come on . . ."

"No, you stop there," Luke defiantly shouted as he turned and pointed his finger at the lawyer, stopping Drew in his tracks. "Keep your distance. I have nothing to say about the note. Get out of here before someone recognizes you," Luke demanded as he fumbled with his keys, trying to enter his car.

Drew stopped and watched as he got in, started the engine, and drove away.

# CHAPTER SIX

**Monday morning**

Drew headed back to the office from his last court appearance of the morning. Turning right onto Fifth Avenue, the black convertible slowed as he approached the Gaslamp Tavern.

*Can't pass up an opportunity to give a smile or wave to the lovely new waitress.*

Sure enough, there was Monica seating a young couple at an outdoor table. Drew tapped his horn ever so gentle and waved. She looked up and responded with a big smile and a wave that said more than hello. At least that was what the young man hoped.

As he pulled into the Ace Parking lot across from his office, Mario ran up.

"Hey, Mario, I met with Miguel."

"Yeah, he told me. You going to represent his father?"

"I talked to Mr. Guerra and agreed to investigate his case. I think I can help him."

"Gracias, Jefe. The family is good people."

Drew flipped Mario the keys and headed to his office. Once he entered, Debbie gestured to the conference room.

"You should talk to Liz. They're going through the De Jesus police file. They have something important to tell you."

"Anything interesting?" Drew asked as he entered the room.

Matt started to say something but Liz spoke up, "They didn't give us much. No internal affairs report on the shooting and the arrest reports are sparse. Frankly, they're no help."

Matt, dying to speak, stood, but Liz gave him a dirty look. The young man remained standing but looked down.

"Drew, here is the summary of our review of the police reports the DA provided on the carjacking," Liz announced forcibly as she handed the packet to Drew.

Drew looked at the small stack of papers in his hand. "Is this what Farrat gave to the judge?"

"No. We got a call from the DA's office. They said we could pick up all discovery directly from the police. They told Debbie nothing was being withheld."

Matt finally couldn't hold back. "I think you should read all the reports . . . carefully."

"Yes, Drew, that's a good idea," Liz injected before Matt could say more. "Then tell us what we should do next." she added while glaring at Matt.

"Thanks, guys. I'll get right to it."

Drew turned and walked back toward his office manager. "Debbie, hold my calls. I want to read these," the lawyer said as he entered his office and shut the door.

With the discovery packet in his lap, Drew sat, feet propped up on his desk, casually going through the carjack transcript of the police dispatch operator and then the five police officers' incident reports. When he got to the report by the officer who initiated the pursuit, he slowed down and began to turn the pages carefully. Suddenly, the young man swiveled his feet off the desk and sat erect in his chair. He flipped back to the first page of the report. There at the bottom of the sheet was the officer's last name and badge number.

With a startled look on his face, Drew pushed the intercom button on the desk phone. "Debbie, get Pat on the phone. Tell him I need to talk, immediately." He hung up without waiting for a reply.

Debbie picked up her phone, noticing the two in the conference room staring at her. She gave them a nod, indicating Drew knew and dialed Pat De Luca.

A few minutes later, she spoke through the intercom, "Drew I have Pat on the phone."

"Put him through."

"Drew, what's the matter?"

"Pat, were you involved in the De Jesus carjacking twenty years ago?"

"Yes. That's why I said I would look into things."

"Why didn't you say so when we talked?"

"I wasn't sure if Guerra was the same guy that was involved in the carjacking."

"Shit, Pat, this complicates things. We need to talk and don't hold back. The reports the DA provided are ridiculously thin. Not your normal felony reports. I need to know everything you know."

"Calm down, Drew. How about this afternoon?"

"Yeah . . . yeah, sure, if that's the quickest you can get here."

"See you at four. Come to think of it, we better meet at the loft. More privacy."

Drew got up from his desk and with the report still in hand opened the door.

"Liz," he yelled, "did you know Pat was involved?"

Both Liz and Matt stepped out from the conference room.

"We weren't sure if the De Luca in the report was Pat or not," she responded.

"That's right," Matt added.

"You got anything else that I should know?"

"No, Drew," she replied.

"Matt, did you make sure they gave us the whole De Jesus file?"

"Yes, sir. I stood there and checked it out and asked if that was all. They said yes."

"Did you specifically ask for the internal investigation file?"

"Absolutely. I said 'Where's the police shooting file' and they said, 'that was all they had.' Did I screw up boss?"

"No, they're just playing games with us. Liz, call the lieutenant who handles discovery and specifically say the judge ordered them to turn over the Internal Affairs report on the shooting."

"Yes, Drew."

"Ah, boss, what about Pat De Luca?" asked Matt.

He ignored Matt's question. "Liz, tell them you also want the names of all officers involved in the arrest and shooting, along with their written reports. This is not how cops handle a police shooting. There's got to be more."

"On it."

Twenty minutes later Liz walked into Drew's office.

"I've got Lieutenant Samson on the line. He says he gave us everything."

"Tell Debbie to send the call in here," he commanded as Drew gestured for Liz to sit and be a part of the call.

When the call came through, he punched a button his desk phone. "Lieutenant Samson, Drew Hawke here."

"Yes, good morning."

"Sir, thanks for taking our call. The judge ordered your department to turn over all reports concerning the De Jesus car theft and shooting. But what you gave us doesn't have any reports dealing with the arrest of Guerra or his interview.

Nor are there reports by the officers involved in the De Jesus brothers shooting. And you didn't give us the Internal Affairs investigation report on the shooting which the judge specifically ordered released."

The lieutenant explained he found no such reports in the De Jesus file.

"But, Lieutenant, that is not normal. Shoots always have an IA investigation."

"Mr. Hawke, this is a twenty-year-old case and any number of things could have happened to the file. I'm not even sure if there was an Internal Affairs investigation."

"I see. Would you look one more time? If you can't find anything more, I may file a motion to dismiss the new murder charges based on the lack of evidence or the spoliation of relevant defense evidence."

"Mr. Hawke, you will have to take that up with the district attorney. I've checked our files, thoroughly, there just isn't anything more."

"Lieutenant, you've been most patient. Thanks for your time."

Drew turned to Liz as he hung up the phone. "Liz, I need you to research and add to our motion to dismiss the failure of the police to preserve necessary evidence which is relevant to the defense. How can there be a trial twenty years later when we don't have all the damn evidence," the exasperated lawyer emphasized with a fist pound on the desk.

"Should I talk to Patrick and ask him if he was involved in the shooting?"

"No. I'll do that."

# CHAPTER SEVEN

## At the loft

Drew kept looking at his phone, which at the moment read: 4:40 p.m. His trusted investigator said he would come by at 4:00. *I hope nothing has happened. Pat's always on time.*

Finally, he heard a knock at the loft door.

"Tami, is that Pat?" Drew asked his computer program.

"Are you inquiring who is knocking at the door?" came the reply.

"Yes, Tami," he replied in an annoyed tone. "I'm expecting Pat."

"There is a man I recognize as Pat De Luca asking to come in."

"Unlock the door and let him," Drew answered, raising his voice, thoroughly frustrated by the delay.

"Have I done something wrong, Drew?"

"Damn!" *The program always responds slowly when I seem angry.* "No, Tami. Pat's just late." *They didn't tell me this artificial intelligence stuff could sense feelings. What's next?*

Drew opened the loft door and greeted Pat. "Sorry for the delay. Tami is a little slow. I'll have to check her programming."

"You and your computer toys," replied Pat.

Drew ignored the attempt at humor and without even

asking his investigator to sit went directly to the meeting's purpose.

"Pat, were you involved in the De Jesus shooting?"

"You got problems with your client?"

"No. I got the police file and your name is mentioned."

"How about we take a seat?"

"Sure. Sorry, it's been a long day," Drew added as he pointed to the couch and chair next to his computer.

"The answer to your question is yes. Twenty years ago, Patrol Officer Thomas Clayton and I were in a carjack pursuit. It involved three young men. One of them was Carlos Guerra, your client. The suspects ran into a road block and fled on foot. Clayton pursued two of them. They were Juan and Manny De Jesus. I followed the third, Carlos Guerra. While chasing Guerra, I heard three shots in a row. I broke off my pursuit and ran toward the shots to back up Clayton. As I ran to Clayton, I heard a fourth shot."

Drew leaned forward as Pat continued.

"When I got to him, both brothers were lying on the ground, shot. Clayton was standing over Manny with his foot on the guy's hand which still held the gun."

"I don't understand."

"Just wait, Drew. Juan De Jesus died at the hospital, one shot to the chest and one to his back. Both Manny and Guerra were charged under the felony murder rule. To avoid the chair, Manny pled to life with the possibility of parole. Manny was killed in a prison riot several years later. Guerra pled to felony carjacking with a ten-year maximum sentence."

"So," asked Drew, "I'm still not sure what all this has to do with my client."

"Here's why. Tom Clayton was part of the Enforcers. Before I was interviewed by Internal Affairs about the shooting, a group of officers approached me and, in no uncertain terms, told me to say nothing about the fourth shot or to reveal anything about the Enforcers. So, I just told Internal Affairs what I saw, nothing more. Interestingly, the investigators never asked me how many shots I heard. Something they would normally do. They had plenty of opportunities to ask during my interview. I never said anything further about the shooting."

"The Blue Code had closed ranks, is that what you're implying?"

"Yes. That's why I left."

"Were there any other witnesses to the shooting?"

"No."

Referring the note he had received earlier, Drew said, "By 'coming after you,' that means . . ."

"They intend to do some bad stuff. Probably kill Guerra. Since I know about the shooting and you represent Guerra, they may even need to get rid of me."

"Pat, I think that threat is more than a possibility. You see, the entire police file on the car theft has been sanitized. There's nothing about how many shots were fired. There's no IA investigation. There aren't even police interviews of Manny and Carlos."

"So I'm the only witness that knows about the four shots."

"Pat, what are we going to do?"

"I need to talk to Chief Shaughnessy and Clayton. They both were involved. But first I have to get Lauren out of town. I don't want her in danger if things turn violent."

"You should go with her."

"No, Drew. Some things you just have to confront head on. If I run, it will confirm I believe Clayton killed Juan. They will just hunt me down. There can't be any loose ends."

"I see. But how is Shaughnessy involved?"

"Shaughnessy was the lieutenant in charge at the time of the shooting. Tony MacNeal, my partner for many years, and at the time a new sergeant, was second in charge. Neither should have been involved in the investigation into the shooting. When I told Shaughnessy there was a suspicious fourth shot, he told me to forget about it and immediately took over the investigation. He even intervened in the Internal Affairs review."

"What's so important about the fourth shot?"

"It occurred several minutes after the first three. When I got there, Manny's gun was still warm; I could tell it had just been fired. More important, Juan was shot twice and Manny took one to the chest."

"Are you saying Clayton planted the gun in Manny's hand?"

"Yes. He probably put the gun in his hand and pulled the trigger in order to justify him shooting the two."

"That makes sense. Guerra said Manny told him he threw his gun away while running."

"That's it, Drew. Clayton told everyone Manny shot first."

"But, Pat, why would they come after Guerra now? It's been so many years. Wait . . . maybe Guerra's been saying things about the shoot."

"That's probably why he's being charged with felony murder. Drew, they want to shut him up. Probably kill him while in prison, just like Manny."

"And I, as Guerra's attorney, will be all over the old shooting as I try to raise a defense for my client. Damn, Pat, you've got to get out of town."

"Can't run. Right now we have to secure our loved ones. I've got to send Lauren to her sister's home in Colorado."

Pat paused, then continued. "And you could be a target, also. You should drop the case and hope they leave you alone."

Silence followed. Pat started to become uncomfortable as

Drew didn't respond to his suggestion. Finally, the young man spoke.

"You know, Pat, I thought I was asking a simple question that could be answered with a yes or no. Instead, your explanation raises a whole other question. Does my job mean I should risk my life to save my client? Personally, I say 'fuck 'em.' If I cower, not only will Guerra be convicted but probably killed like Manny De Jesus. Realistically, I think the Enforcers have already made the decision for me and even you."

"What do you mean?"

"I'm sure they believe Carlos told me everything. If the Enforcers are out to silence witnesses, like Carlos and you, my dropping the case won't work."

Still thinking about Drew's safety, Pat asked, "Answer me this: How did the man get up here and slip the note under your door? I thought no one could enter the elevator, much less ride it to your floor, without your okay."

"I'm afraid I got lax. Actually, I just got lazy. I had turned off the security system. All he had to do is take the elevator up to the loft door."

"Turn on the security system and keep it on."

"I will."

"And, Drew, I want to know the security codes in case of an emergency."

"Don't worry. I already programmed the system so your index finger on the elevator scanner will still activate the elevator and your eye will open the loft door. I got rid of the keypad system months ago. I just have to keep the system on."

"Good. Now we have to tell your staff. They have to know what's going on. Do you agree?"

"I don't know if I should. It may scare them, even cause them to quit."

"Debbie, Liz, and Matt are as much a part of the case as you. The Enforcers will assume they know what you know."

"What a mess."

"Drew, when your action puts people in danger, you have to tell them and let them decide if they wish to stay."

"You're right. I'll tell them."

"Why not let me do that with you. They should know the whole story."

"Okay, tomorrow morning."

Pat started to rise when Drew spoke. "The way you're talking, you think you can handle this on your own. It seems we are in this together. I insist on being involved."

"I'll think about that."

"No, Pat. I mean it. We are stronger together."

Pat nodded but Drew was convinced Pat didn't think so. The two men embraced and walked to the elevator.

Pat started to open the loft door but Drew touched his arm. "Pat, if Shaughnessy did what you said, he must be an Enforcer. Am I correct?"

"Can't say for sure."

"Let's assume he is. If Shaughnessy is part of the gang, shouldn't the mayor know about the Enforcers?"

"Doubtful, Drew. Sam Sandleson wasn't mayor when the Enforcers were active."

Drew insisted on riding down with Pat to make sure he got to his car safely. As Pat drove away, Drew said a prayer, asking God to protect the only man who has cared for him—deservedly the man Drew called "father."

As Drew rode the elevator back to the loft, he shook his head. *I don't think Pat's going to involve me.* Once inside the loft, Drew sat trying to figure out what to do.

"Tami, I need to talk to Mario Rodriquez. Text him using the urgent emoji."

A few minutes later Mario called.

"Tami, speaker on."

"Mario, I'm at the loft. I need your help. Can you come over?"

"On my way."

Once Mario arrived, the two sat as Drew explained why Mr. Guerra was in real trouble and how Drew's investigator had been threatened.

"Drew, I'm sorry I asked you to help Miguel and his father."

"No, you did the right thing. Any idea how you can help me protect Pat without him knowing? I think he's going to keep me out of the loop."

Mario smiled. "Sí, I have this friend. He's real good at electronics. He will know what to do."

"Good idea. Can we see him tonight?"

"Let me call."

An hour later, Mario's friend showed up. A Hispanic man dressed in an expensive-looking, Chino-style beige pant, sporting a black Darth Vader T-shirt, and black Diego leather sneakers. The causally dressed twenty-something carried a large briefcase.

"Compadre," Mario greeted enthusiastically. "This is my amigo, abogado Andrew Hawke. He's the hombre I told you about. He's a good friend. Mr. Hawke helped me get off parole once I got out of prison. He cleared my record so I could get a good job."

The young lawyer extended his hand to the guest. "I'm Drew. Ah, Mario didn't tell me your name."

"Good evening, Mr. Hawke, I'm Julian Ramirez, nice to meet you."

"Mario didn't tell me what you do."

"I'm a computer engineer."

"Jefe, he works for Celestecom. A big company."

"We develop software and design semiconductor chips for our parent company."

"The big semiconductor and wireless communication company here in San Diego?" Drew asked.

"Yes, sir."

"He used to work for the CIA."

"Mario, that was a long time ago."

"CIA?" Drew asked.

"Yes, and later the FBI."

"You look young. What did you do for them."

"I am twenty-seven, Mr. Hawke. But I was seventeen when the CIA recruited me."

"He hacked the government's computers, Jefe."

"Mario, I don't tell people about that."

"Don't worry, Julian, I'm an attorney. I don't talk about people or their past. But what exactly did you do for the FBI?"

"The same I did for the CIA. I designed their computer security systems and ran programs to counter foreign hackers."

"Wow, Julian. Where have you been hiding? I could use your skills for my pathetic security system and Tami, that's the AI program I designed."

"Yes, Drew. How may I help you?"

"Tami, go to sleep."

"Shutting down."

"Sorry, guys, I forgot she was on voice activation."

"Cool," Julian said, walking over to the computer. She sounds fun. What does Tami do?"

"It runs everything in the loft for me."

"Maybe I could look at it later."

"Sure. But, Julian, I hate to ask a thousand questions, but why did you leave such an important job for the private sector?"

"That's okay, Drew. I understand. I was recruited by Celestecom. They offered money I couldn't turn down."

"Julian is a good man, Jefe. His family needed help."

Julian looked at Mario and tried to change the subject. "Mario said you are in deep trouble."

"Oh, yes, I'm in a world of hurt."

Without going into details or saying anything about the Enforcers, Drew described how he wanted to follow his investigator and, if necessary, come to his aid.

"Are the police involved?"

"No, they can't be. Nor can my investigator know I am watching. He specifically told me not to get involved."

Julian spoke in Spanish to Mario and then turned to Drew. "Not to offend you, sir, but Mario told me these are bad cops who want to kill your man. How are you going to stop them? Do you have a gun?"

"No. I don't own a gun, but I can get one."

Julian again spoke in Spanish to Mario before responding. "Mr. Hawke, I am an electronic surveillance expert. What you are attempting to do is watch someone twenty-four seven. No one can stay awake twenty-four hours a day. To kill a man takes only seconds. You need help."

"Julian, I'm young. I'll find a way."

"Mr. Hawke, I designed satellite and mobile surveillance programs for the FBI, but even with such tech assistance they needed agents in the field as well as people monitoring my programs. You just can't do this alone."

Mario interrupted and again the two conversed in Spanish.

"Mario says he and some friends could help. But, Mr.

Hawke, Mario is an ex-felon, like my brother, and they can't possess a gun. Somebody is going to get killed, either you or one of them."

"Julian, I'll take my chances. But you're right, I can't involve other people."

Mario started to speak and Drew interrupted him. "No, Mario, Julian is right.

"But Jefe . . ."

"No, Mario. This is a bad idea. Besides, I also need to protect my office staff. I think the best thing I can do is close my office.

"But, Mr. Hawke, I not afraid to die."

As if not hearing Mario, Drew offered his hand. "Mr. Ramirez, thank you for coming. I appreciate the sound advice."

Drew escorted the two to the loft elevator. As the elevator started down, Drew was at a loss of what to do next.

At the parking lot, Julian and Mario spoke in Spanish, then Julian turned to Drew.

"Mr. Hawke, Mario is right we can help. Let us at least explain."

Drew nodded.

# CHAPTER EIGHT

**Tuesday morning**

Drew sat at the head of the conference table. Present were Debbie and Liz to the left of Drew, with Pat and Matt to his right.

Drew's private investigator looked at the three employees, who seemed unsure why they were there. "I'm going to tell you something and none of you can tell anyone else. If you do, you will put your lives in danger and possibly the rest of us."

Debbie immediately spoke up. "Drew Hawke, what have you done?"

"Drew has done nothing, Debbie. Let me explain. When I was a police officer, there existed a criminal element within the San Diego Police Department. At the time, many police officers literally took justice into their own hands. As a result, some suspects were brutalized and others executed. This group called themselves the Enforcers. I left the department because I could not condone such extra-judicial acts. Your Guerra case was one such execution."

Matt rocked back in his chair onto its two hind legs and folded his arms. Everyone else remained attentive as Pat continued.

"Friday night, following Drew's fight at the Sheraton, a note was slipped under his loft door. The note warned Drew the

Enforcers were coming after me. The reason I am threatened is because I am a witness who might say Tom Clayton was a member of the Enforcers when he shot Juan and Manny De Jesus."

"Why would they think you would talk?" asked Matt as he rocked forward onto all four legs of his chair.

"I'm close to Drew and everyone knows I work for him. Now that Drew represents Guerra, the assumption will be I have told Drew about the shooting and the existence of the Enforcers."

All three of the staff started to speak but Drew interrupted.

"Guys, the reason we are telling you this is because you work for me. Your lives could very well be in danger."

The three loyal employees leaned back in their chairs in shock. Silence momentarily filled the room.

"Debbie . . . Liz . . . Matt." Drew slowly called out each name, pausing while holding his gaze on each one individually. I am giving you two months' severance pay while you look for a new job. If you need more I will assist you further."

Matt didn't even wait to raise his hand. "You firing us?"

"I think it best you distance yourself from this mess and go on with your lives," he replied.

"Uh-uh. I ain't goin' nowhere," Debbie said in the most forceful manner Drew had ever heard.

"Boss, you staying in the Guerra case?" Matt asked.

"Yes, Matt."

"Drew, how can we go? There's other clients and the Guerra motions," Liz said.

"I think you should leave for your own safety. I'll find other attorneys to take over the cases."

"I think you underestimate us Drew Hawke," replied the associate attorney.

"Damn right," Matt exclaimed in a rising voice. "You expect us to run. No way. But I will have to get a gun."

"Matt, you don't even know how to use a gun," Drew protested. "You'll just end up harming yourself."

"Wait a minute," interrupted Pat. "Let's back up and think rationally. Drew is right. Things can get very dangerous for him and, by extension, possibly for you. Understanding this, let's talk about what has to be done to close the firm."

Liz was the first to speak up. "One year, possibly two, to close all the cases. We've got about fifty cases. Even if you gave the cases to other attorneys, it would take us weeks, maybe months, to brief every case properly for another attorney."

"I agree," Matt added.

"I ain't leavin'," Debbie said. "You may as well get that through your thick head, Andrew Hawke."

"Guys," Drew injected, "you should leave. I appreciate your dedication, but we are dealing with a life-and-death situation. I intend to close the office."

In a loud voice, Debbie added, "How many are stayin'?"

Before Drew could say more, his phone vibrated. "Excuse me just a second, guys." Drew looked at the text message. Debbie and Liz looked at each other as if asking how could he take a text message at this time. Drew ignored the looks. Finally, he put down the phone.

"Okay. If you want to stay, raise your hands."

All three raised their hands.

"Boss, I'm going to get a gun," Matt said.

Pat again spoke up calmly. "If you insist on being foolish, Matt, please let me take you to a firing range and show you how to safely handle a gun. At least how to hit what you aim at."

Much to Pat's surprise, Matt leaned over and hugged him. "Thanks, man."

Drew's phone vibrated once more. Another Mario text. The message read, "tracking device attached."

As everyone rose, Drew motioned for the staff to sit as he walked Pat out of the office. A few moments later, he returned and shut the conference room door.

"Look, guys, I really understand your desire to keep us open, but I have to tell you again, you got to go. I have to help protect Pat, so there won't be much legal work being done until this whole thing is over."

Debbie rose and announced, "I've got a lot of work to do, excuse me."

With that Liz and Matt stood. "Excuse us too, Drew."

Drew just sat there, not knowing what to do. A thousand different thoughts ran through his mind.

*Well, I guess that's that,* he concluded. *No, this whole thing is too dangerous. They could get caught in the crossfire if Clayton comes for Pat and me. Yup, that's how it will go down. Pat knows I will be by his side.* After a few moments, *Nah, Clayton won't come alone, he's a fucking coward, there'll be others. Maybe at the office, late in the afternoon or when we work late into the early evening. I can't have Debbie and the others in danger. As for Pat, doubtful they'll try to get him here. It's more likely the Enforcers will come for Pat at night when no one's around. No witnesses that way. I just can't risk it. Debbie, Liz, and Matt have to leave.*

Drew's confusion grew as his reasoning went in circles. *No way. Debbie will just sit at her desk, even if there's no work. She is so stubborn. I can hear her now, "When your Mumma was dying, she made me promise to look after you. That's how it is. Yes, sir, I is stayin." She'll never leave me, that's her way.*

Drew finally rose and exited the conference room without saying a word to anyone as he went into his office and shut the door. Drew turned on his office stereo and sat at his desk in deep thought. *Mario and Julian's new idea will not be enough,* Drew reasoned as he went back over their late-night strategy he had finally agreed to. *I shouldn't have allowed them to come back up. Nor should I have agreed to their plan. The plan could only work if it was only Pat. But not closing the office . . . it just won't work. Knowing where Pat and the rest of the staff is all the time isn't enough. I could be minutes away, precious minutes, before I could get to them. Yup, Julian's surveillance technology is just an alert system. It will not protect so many people at once. Julian was right. I need people on the ground. I need help.*

There he sat for the better part of an hour, sometimes getting up and walking around, starring out the window, and back to the desk.

"Finnigan! Finnigan Macintosh," the lawyer yelled as he got up and picked up his backpack lying on the floor next to his gym bag. He unzipped it and fumbled around inside until he found the battery extender Finnigan gave him following the Pansky case victory. Drew plugged the extender into the bottom of his cell phone. The attorney hesitated a second as he looked at the phone. *I need help.* He pushed the star key just as Finnigan had told him to. The phone automatically dialed CIA Agent Finnigan Macintosh.

The phone rang many times, and just before Drew was going to hang up he heard a voice. "Drew, I'm glad you called. I have been talking to Katherine Pansky about you."

"Finnigan, you still exploiting her?"

"That's a rather harsh description. But yes, Senator Katherine Pansky is working for us."

"Where is she?"

"On a mission. The Chinese supposedly have her getting

something important for them, but they're really testing her to see if Katherine is connected enough to spy for them like her husband did. Have you decided to help her?"

"No. But I need your advice."

"It must be important for you to call me. Go ahead. What is it?"

"I got myself into a mess that involves a San Diego Police Department gang called the Enforcers. Have you heard about them?"

When he got no response, Drew spoke up, "Fin, Finnigan!"

"Drew, that is a strange question. Why do you ask?"

"They are threatening to kill my private investigator and, by extension, my staff, possibly me, in order to cover up a twenty-year-old murder of a suspect by a police officer."

"Is this one of your cases?"

"Yes."

"Drew, I think it best we continue our conversation on a secure government line at the U.S. Attorney's Office. You, and you alone, call U.S. Attorney Wyland and arrange a time late this afternoon, say around 4:00 p.m. I'll have to get to my embassy so we can talk. This afternoon your time will work perfectly. I will call you then."

"Absolutely."

"Good. Use your phone with the extender plugged in when you call Wyland. Do as I instructed, push the star key but then immediately type 00593. Your phone will automatically be directed to Wyland's office. You will be on a protected line, secure from electronic surveillance or hacking."

"Spooky stuff, Finnigan."

"No, Drew, what you are involved in is spooky stuff."

# CHAPTER NINE

At 3:30 p.m., Drew walked into the United States Federal Building in downtown San Diego. He was early but didn't want to be late. The lawyer knew he needed help, and Finnigan was his best hope. As Drew exited the elevator on the floor for the office of the United States Attorney for Southern California, Drew wondered what an electronic safe room would look like.

He paused at the door, then entered the office.

"Good afternoon. I'm Drew Hawke."

"Oh, yes, Mr. Hawke," replied a well-dressed, middle-aged woman. "Just a second please." The woman picked up her phone. "Sir, Mr. Hawke is here. . . . Yes, he is early." She hung up and directed Hawke to follow. After walking through an interior office, she opened the door to the office of U.S. Attorney Oliver T. Wyland.

"Mr. Hawke, what a pleasant surprise. Nice to see you again."

Wyland motioned for his secretary to close the door.

"Thank you, sir, for letting Mr. Macintosh and me use your offices."

"Have a seat, Hawke. May I call you Drew?"

"Of course, Oly."

Wyland smiled as he remembered their previous encounter

where Wyland told the young attorney to call him by his first name.

"I see the roles are now reversed from our previous meeting," said the U.S. attorney with a smirk.

"I thought I was to talk by secure phone to Macintosh."

"Oh, yes. No need. I told Finnigan I would handle things."

*Oh, shit. What in the world is the man going to demand of me?* thought Drew.

"If that's so, Oly, what price must I pay for your advice?"

Wyland laughed out loud. "Young man, you simply amaze me with your directness."

"I was hoping you would say intuitiveness," replied Drew.

"You know, Drew, you have a way of taking the fun out of things." The man smiled. "Nevertheless, I am the one who can help you."

"How so?"

"You told Finnigan your investigator has received a death threat from a corrupt gang of police officers because of one of your cases."

"Um-hm."

"The FBI has been investigating corruption in San Diego for several years. If what you told Finnigan is accurate, then the corruption extends into the police. So how about you tell us what you know."

"I hate bad cops, so yes. The police officers who are threatening my people are apparently part of a group called the Enforcers. They are coming after my investigator and possibly my staff. I need you to protect him and my law staff."

"I wasn't aware the Enforcers still existed."

"Sir, I never heard of them until Pat told me about them this weekend."

"Who is Pat?"

"Pat De Luca, my investigator. The one those bad cops want to kill."

"Tell me more."

"First, I want a deal."

"Deal. I think the shoe is on the other foot this time. I'm not the one wanting something. You came to me for help. So I will decide whatever deal is to be made."

"In that case, Mr. Wyland, good afternoon." Drew got up and started for the office door.

"Damn it, Hawke you are one stubborn, hard-driving son-of-a-bitch."

Hawke stopped, turned around, and in a strong voice said, "Sir, I may be all that but one way or another, I will take care of my own people, with or without your help."

Oly laughed. "Finnigan told me you would be a handful. Frankly, you're more than that. What do you want?"

Drew walked back but remained standing. He put both hands on the large ornate desk and leaned forward. "Pat De Luca and my staff have to be protected. I also need your help with a plan to put those Enforcers out of business so they can't come after my friends again. I don't know how."

"And you are one of those needing protection?"

"No, I can take care of myself."

Wyland smiled and pointed to the side chair in front of his desk. "Sit down."

Drew sat down and waited while Wyland pressed the intercom button on his phone. "Send him in." The door opened and in walked someone Drew knew.

"Special Agent Kiefer Mancini, I believe you know Mr. Hawke."

"Yes, I do. Attorney Hawke, good day," the tall FBI agent said, extending his hand in greeting as Drew rose.

"Mr. Hawke has walked into a hornet's nest of corrupt cops and needs our help," Oliver Wyland lamented, this time dead serious.

"Is this part of our San Diego investigation we talked about?" the agent asked.

"Yes. My intuition tells me these Enforcers will somehow lead us to the corrupt officials we now have under surveillance."

"I see."

"My apologies, Kiefer, please be seated."

"Thank you, sir. Mr. Wyland, what exactly does Mr. Hawke know?"

"I thought it best you be present when he tells us what's going on."

"My friends, Mr. Wyland," Drew said, "how are you going to ensure they won't be harmed?"

"Ah, yes. Kiefer, Mr. Hawke needs security for his investigator and employees. Finnigan said death threats have been made. We've provided such security in the past, but here Hawke is asking us to protect those who make his law office function. Your advice?"

"Drew," Agent Mancini responded, "closing your office and hiding everyone would just make this gang of officers suspicious. Worse, if they figure out the FBI is involved, they may resort to methods much harder to prevent." The agent paused, knowing what he was about to say was always distressing to a lay person.

"If their intent is to kill, it would be easier if they just resorted to a long-range sniper shot. So, I recommend we keep the office open during the day."

Drew squirmed in his chair and had a shocked look on his face.

Seeing Drew's obvious alarm at leaving his friends sitting

ducks, Wyland intervened. "Drew, we want to engage these Enforcers somehow so we can get incriminating evidence on what they're up to. That really is the best way to put them away for good."

"Exactly," added Mancini. "Agent Macintosh told me the person they have threatened is your investigator, an ex-San Diego officer, who is working on one of your cases. Is that correct?"

"Finnigan told you, too?"

Agent Mancini looked at Wyland, who nodded slightly.

"I was on the call with Oly."

Drew looked at Wyland. "I see." Inside he was furious. *The ass lied to me again. Fin told them everything.*

"Yes, Finnigan is correct," Drew said. "Pat De Luca has been threatened. But I am also fearful for Debbie, Liz, and Matt, who may also be in danger, especially if you want me to keep the office open."

"I understand," Kiefer said reassuringly. "Here's what we normally do when others might become targets. I suggest we put one of our agents in your office and assign agents to surveil each individual employee when they are out of the office. Your office is small enough so we can do that. This helps to keep them from being taken hostages in order to get to you or Mr. De Luca."

Noting the young attorney's confused look, Wyland interrupted again. "Drew, this is a good idea. If these crooked officers can't get to you or De Luca, they will grab one of your employees in order to force you and Pat to cooperate."

"Grab?"

"Yes. But, Drew, look at me," demanded Wyland. "If they can keep De Luca and you silent without kidnapping or killing someone, that, frankly, is the cleanest way to proceed. These men are not stupid. They are used to intimidating people to get their way. Threatening someone with a note or phone call is at this time the best way to proceed."

"I'm sorry to be blunt," Drew replied, "but you appear to be using Pat and my office staff as bait."

"No," objected Wyland. "Quite the opposite. We want these Enforcers to engage and impose the police officers' code of silence which Finnigan believes De Luca has adhered to these many years."

"So you two think the Enforcers intend to keep Pat silent rather than killing him?"

"That would be the smartest way for them to proceed. Killing a fellow officer, or even a retired officer who has kept his mouth shut, would be a dangerous precedence since their whole code is based on a trust within the Brotherhood."

"Guys, this whole plan of yours is based on this fraternity of blue and its bullshit code of silence. The ones with the most to lose are Detective Clayton and Chief Shaughnessy. They could care less about this code shit. They're thinking about their hides."

Agent Mancini and Wyland exchanged surprised looks. Kiefer spoke first.

"Those are the ones making the threats?"

"Pat thinks Clayton killed a suspect and Shaughnessy covered up the shooting back when they were patrol officers. Thomas Clayton and Pat De Luca were pursuing three car thieves. A foot chase ensured. The suspects split up. Clayton went after two and Pat after the third. Pat heard three shots in a row, so he stopped and ran to Clayton. As he did, Pat heard a fourth shot minutes later. Upon arriving at the scene, Pat saw the two suspects on the ground. Both had been shot. Pat thinks a gun was planted to justify Clayton shooting them.

Shaughnessy was the lieutenant in charge of the carjack pursuit and the shooting investigation. You'll have to talk to Pat about all this."

"All this happened when?" asked Kiefer.

"Twenty years ago. Back then a group of the Enforcers told Pat to say nothing about the shooting. Shortly thereafter, he left the police department because he didn't want to be part of the police gang."

"Did he ever tell anyone about this?"

"Kiefer, I don't think so. Pat just told me yesterday after I got the note saying the Enforcers were coming after him."

"What note?" asked Wyland.

"Yesterday someone slipped a note under my loft door. Here—"

Drew reached into his pocket and handed it to Wyland. After reading it Wyland handed it Agent Mancini.

"Who wrote this?" asked Kiefer. "It's unsigned."

"I'm not sure. But the evening before I fought a police officer in a sanctioned cage fight at the Sheraton Hotel. The note reads like he wrote it. See here? 'You're a good man. I had to tell you.' 'You're a good man.' Those are the exact words Luke D'Angelo told me when we hugged in the cage after I knocked him out. The note says I shouldn't have taken the case. That is Carlos Guerra, who was the suspect Pat De Luca was chasing," Drew explained. "The De Jesus brothers were the ones Clayton shot. The older brother, Juan, died at the hospital, and Manny, the younger one, went to prison under the felony murder rule for his brother's death."

Drew paused as he took a deep breath and resumed. "Guerra told me Manny was telling fellow prisoners Clayton was on the take and that he shot the brothers after they surrendered. Guerra also said Manny had thrown away the gun used in the carjack as they ran from Clayton. All of a sudden, twenty years later, Guerra has been charged for Juan's death under the same felony murder rule. He's been out of prison for sixteen years."

"Is Carlos Guerra your client?"

"Yes. I'm trying to defend him against this old felony murder charge."

U.S. Attorney Wyland, fully erect in his seat, asserted himself. "Drew, you indeed are in the middle of a nasty mess. I do believe your investigator and, by extension you and your staff, are in danger. Whether they kill Mr. De Luca depends on him convincing them he won't talk. If they don't believe him, they will kill him. You may be next if they think you know too much about the old killing."

Wyland rose and walked around his desk to Drew. "Here's what I want you to do. Go with Kiefer and let him tell you his plan to get these crooks and protect your friends. We've done this many times before. We are good at what we do. Not cooperating will be the biggest mistake of your life and, regrettably, will probably endanger your friends' lives."

Drew Hawke sat in silence, thinking. Finally, he said to agent Mancini, "Okay, let's talk. I called Agent Macintosh because I don't know what to do. So let's talk."

"Good decision," Wyland said as he extended his hand. "Go with Mancini. He has a team waiting to talk to you."

"You planned to help all along, didn't you, Oly?"

"Drew, your situation is only part of a bigger one we have been working on for years. Yes, we know a lot more than we're saying. You will be filled in as things progress. Right now, you just have to go with the flow and trust us. We are the ones you need."

# CHAPTER TEN

**Monday, 4:25 p.m.**

Agent Mancini escorted Drew down a long corridor, through a private office, and into a large room full of FBI personnel. All rose as the two walked in.

Drew looked around the room. Two of the walls were covered in photographs of his employees and himself, of his office interior, nearby office buildings, and both ground and aerial shots of the outsides of each of his friends' homes and apartments. The young man stared at it all as he realized Wyland had truly not been truthful about what he knew.

"Ladies and gentlemen, this is attorney Andrew Hawke, the case we have been preparing for since this morning. Drew, this is our crisis team. Please let me introduce Dr. Powell. Doctor, please step forward. Dr. F. Simon Powell is one of our specialists."

A thin man in a long-sleeved blue shirt and appropriately matched tie approached and shook Drew's hand.

"Dr. Powell is a department psychologist," explained Mancini.

"Nice to meet you, Doctor."

"Actually, Mr. Hawke, I'm a criminal behavioral expert. One of my areas of expertise is police behavior and why officers abuse suspects and commit crimes themselves."

"Dr. Powell also helps the Bureau analyze crime scenes and profile suspects," Mancini added. "In your case, he is advising us on the best way to deal with the Enforcers."

"I assume, Doctor, you believe the police officers in this matter would prefer to enforce their code of silence instead of killing my investigator," stated Hawke.

"Actually, yes," responded the expert as he removed his glasses. Holding them in his hand, he gestured toward Drew. "You see, killing someone at this stage of their effort to cover up a twenty-year-old murder would raise too many questions. Now, eliminating Mr. Guerra at a later date, well that's another question."

Kiefer interrupted. "Drew, we will get into all this in a few minutes. First, let's have a seat." He pointed to two seats at the front of the room. "Agent Jakub Nowak, please brief Mr. Hawke on our preliminary thoughts on how to protect him, his staff, and Pat De Luca. Jakub, the floor is yours."

"Mr. Hawke, we would normally protect an asset by moving them to a safe house or, if their time with us, let's say as a witness, is short, we would put them up in a hotel suite with agents. However, in your case, we have several members of your office to protect. Complicating things is you have a very well know law practice, which should be kept open."

"Agent Nowak."

"Yes, Mr. Hawke?"

"Why should I keep my practice open? My idea is to close it and send my staff away. If they work for someone else, they should be safe."

Doctor Powell stood. "Possibly, yes. But you and Mr. De Luca are their threat. Put yourself in the shoes of the Enforcers. If they wish to shut you up, how would they do it?"

"Kill me."

"Why do that when they can threaten those closest to you? Pat De Luca and his wife, Lauren, helped your mother raise you, as did Debra McCaleb. Wouldn't you do anything to protect them?"

Drew folded his arms and sat back in his chair. *How do they know so much about me and my family?*

"If so, Mr. Hawke," continued the expert, "closing your office accomplishes nothing."

Nowak added to the point. "This is why we had agents watching Mr. and Mrs. De Luca right after Macintosh talked to U.S. Attorney Wyland. In fact, we followed them the next day to the airport, determining where Mrs. De Luca was flying and had agents waiting to shadow her to her sister's home. We currently have agents watching the two twenty-four seven."

"Are you watching Pat, too?"

"Yes. But he doesn't know it."

"How do you know so much about my friends?"

Agent Mancini spoke, "Drew your life is a little more complicated than you realize. We know all about you, the De Lucas, and Mrs. McCaleb. If you let us go on, a lot more will become clearer and all your questions will be answered."

Drew just sat mute. *What the hell is going on? Why do they keep saying it will all become clear? Why all the mystery?*

Before the young man could ask another question, Mancini told Nowak to proceed.

"I know, Mr. Hawke, your primary worry is Mr. De Luca—"

Drew interrupted Nowak. "Since you folks know so much about me and my friends, don't you think we can be on a first-name basis? Call me Drew."

Somewhat surprised, Jakub answered, "Yes, sir."

Not waiting, Drew persisted. "So how do you protect Pat De Luca or for that matter, Carlos Guerra?"

Mancini got up and walked over and stood next to Nowak. "We think the best way to protect Guerra is for us to take over the prosecution of his murder case. By asserting prosecutorial jurisdiction, we get Guerra into our custody. We don't think he is safe in the county jail. We just don't know how widespread the Enforcers' influence is in San Diego law enforcement."

Agent Nowak added, "This way, Drew, we can concentrate on protecting you folks and give us time to plan the takedown of the Enforcers. Our objective is to eliminate this criminal element within San Diego law enforcement."

"You're saying Guerra will be safe in your custody," questioned the lawyer.

"Absolutely. We have a safe house on the eastern edge of Camp Pendleton. It's a gated compound with three adjacent structures that can house as many agents as needed. Agents protect the area twenty-four seven. The entire compound is under camera surveillance, with fence and ground sensors. Nobody does anything without us knowing."

"It's where we keep cartel leaders when we prosecute them," added Mancini.

Drew replied, "I think you're missing the full picture. Carlos Guerra has to be free to work. He has a family to provide for. I can get him released."

Suddenly, a voice came from behind Hawke, "Drew, you won't be able to represent Guerra."

Drew turned and looked back. "Liberty Jala, why are you here?"

"Drew, you can't remain Guerra's attorney. You have a conflict," repeated the Assistant U.S. Attorney.

"I disagree, Liberty,"

"Your investigator has been threatened and by extension you and your staff. The very fact you are here asking for help shows you fear your close friends may be harmed. The question then arises, would you put your closest friends before the interests of your client?"

"It is a potential conflict, yes. But I can discuss it with Carlos and get him to waive the conflict."

"Your conflict is deeper than that," came another familiar voice from the back.

Drew looked to the right of Jala. "Wyland! You know, I've had enough of you manipulating me. You haven't told the truth since I first met you a year ago, even more so now. Here you are telling me to abandon my client and let you prosecute him. I'm out of here." Drew rose to leave, anger written all over his face.

"Drew, your father, your biological father is involved."

"My father?" Drew said, stunned as he swung around to face Wyland.

"Yes. He's not dead. He is alive."

Drew had a blank expression as he stared at the U.S. attorney. His words didn't seem to fully register with Hawke in a room that had gone totally silent.

"The city's corruption runs deeper than just the Enforcers. What we have been investigating is a group of local powerbrokers and government officials."

"What's that got to do with . . . my father?"

"One of those city officials is the chief of police, James Shaughnessy. What you told us indicates a possible strong connection between the Enforcers and the city's corrupt officials."

"I still don't see how that affects me and the problem of protecting my investigator and staff."

"We have been trying to figure out how these corrupt officials impose their will on other elected officials, even state judges."

"You're avoiding the question, Wyland. So what!"

Everybody in the room had their eyes fixed on Wyland. He rose and made his way toward Drew. "Let's talk. You should know how your father is involved."

Mancini reached over and gently touched Drew's arm. Drew immediately jerked it away.

"Drew, come with us," the agent whispered. "This is what I've been talking about. You have to know who he is and why we are investigating him."

Drew ignored Mancini, looking at Wyland as the man walked up to him.

"Why are you doing this? I really don't want to know."

Kiefer whispered something in Drew's ear. Drew looked at the agent, turned, and slowly walked with Mancini toward the office they had previously walked through. The expression on his face, his entire demeanor, reflected great angst, if not confusion, as if he didn't know what to do. Once in the office, Wyland pointed to a chair. "Please sit."

A strange feeling gripped him. Drew felt cold all of a sudden. He just shook his head.

"Your biological father is a judge here in San Diego."

Those words reverberated in Hawke's head over and over.

Wyland extended his hand to his right. "Ms. Jala, it's time."

Liberty reached into a thin manila folder and handed Wyland a sheet of paper.

"Here is a certified copy of your birth certificate," Wyland said as he rose and extended it to the stunned young man.

Drew just stared at it, not sure if he wanted it. Wyland shoved the certificate into Drew's hand and closed his fingers around it. As Drew looked at his hand, a whole way of life flashed before him. *My happy childhood. Why do I want to spoil it by finding out those I love lied to me?*"

He slowly raised the paper and began to unfold it, only to start tearing it to shreds as Wyland, Jala, and Mancini watched in shock. Drew threw the ripped pieces to the floor.

"Oly, what do you want from me?"

"Drew, I don't mean to hurt you, but we need you. I have to tell you about your father if we are to get these bastards. Please sit."

"You know, Oly, I have only one father, Pat De Luca. He helped my mother raise me. He's been the only man in my life since I can remember. I don't want to know the name of some son-of-a-bitch that got my mother pregnant."

"Fair enough. But, Drew, I think these crooked officials may be tied to the threat against Mr. De Luca. Please hear us out. We can help protect you and everyone else."

Hawke walked over to the leather chair facing Wyland and slowly sank into it. There he sat, as if the chair had wrapped itself around him.

"Drew, look at me," demanded the U.S. attorney. We've been investigating San Diego Mayor Sam Sandleson, his chief of staff and political strategist, William Bodsly, and various judges." Wyland paused, then pointedly added, "And Chief of Police James Shaughnessy. All these men are tied together by money they've used their power to get. That includes one of the wealthiest men in San Diego, Morgan Mayfield. Through Mayfield's hotel conglomerate, contracts for development of an unusually large number of hotels, business centers, and residential developments have been approved by the city. Controversial building projects, which faced strong local opposition, just sailed through San Diego City Hall. Always backed by Sandleson. When there is an obstacle, judges make favorable rulings. We also think police intimidation is used to get things done. The profits from those projects seem to find their way into offshore bank accounts in the Caribbean. Bank accounts owned by five individuals. Those men are a judge—your father—the mayor, his chief of staff, the police chief, and Mayfield."

"Why tell me all this?"

"Until you came to us about a group of corrupt police officers, we didn't know how to get to this group of five. But the Guerra case gives us the opening to get something on police Detective Thomas Clayton and Chief Shaughnessy. That, we hope, will give us a chance to leverage one or both of the two into a plea deal where they tell us how those business deals got approved. More important, how the group got paid and where the money is."

"You intentionally upended my life, tell me I am related to an unethical crook, so you might have a chance to get evidence," Drew said in a slow sarcastic voice. "You son-of-a-bitch," he yelled as he sat erect in his seat. The anger evident as he shook his head.

"Oly . . . you can shove your investigation where the sun don't shine."

Drew started to rise only to hear Liberty say, "You leave, Drew,, and you sign the death warrant for Guerra and probably for the person you call 'father,' Pat De Luca."

"Drew," spoke Mancini in a soft voice, "think of those you call family. This is not just about you."

Drew settled back into his chair. "You know, you two," Drew said, pointing at Liberty and then looking at Mancini, "you are just as bad as your boss."

Wyland rose and stood looking down on Drew. "Hawke," the U.S. attorney said in a commanding voice, "we are beyond personal feelings. We all have to do our jobs. That includes you, Mr. Attorney. Now please go with Agent Mancini."

As Drew and Mancini returned to the room full of FBI agents, Kiefer pulled Drew aside. In a low voice he said, "Don't mention the bank accounts in the Caribbean."

"Why?"

"At least not now. All our agents are compartmentalized. Each one only has certain information. The agents you met don't know about the money or who your father is. If there is a need to know, then I can show you the bank information."

"I, Kiefer, have a strong need to know. So let's have it. Where in the Caribbean?"

"Okay, okay, I'll talk to Wyland."

# CHAPTER ELEVEN

## The Artful Dodger

Drew didn't go to the loft after the torture session with the Feds. He needed a place of refuge and quiet, away from everyone. But even the Artful Dodger, his 35-foot sailboat, didn't provide solace. He tossed and turned the whole night. What disturbed him so was within his mind. No matter where one goes or what one does, your thoughts will always follow you. To the young, experiencing life with all its ups and downs, it is the uncertainty of life that haunts them day and night. Drew was a man used to controlling things. He could take risks and only he would bear the consequences. But now only others could prevent harm to his loved ones. He was totally at the mercy of very powerful people.

The young lawyer kicked the blankets back. *Why? Why am I surrounded by lies? And why does it have to be him, a crook. My father, an unethical crook. Is this the reason Mom, Pat, and Lauren—even Debbie—told me he was dead? Do I really need to know more about the man who fathered me?"*

Drew got up, yawned, stretched his arms and twisted his stiff, tense back. He looked at his phone: 4:28 a.m.

"This has to stop. I need to know why." He sighed. Slowly he stepped into the main cabin and sat at the dining room table, his head in his hands. After a few minutes, he got up and rummaged through the Dodger's refrigerator. *Nothing but beer and guacamole. No food, not even chips. I gotta remember to shop.*

Finally, he came to a decision. "I will confront Pat and find out why he lied about my father," Drew said out loud. Hearing himself say it helped him believe he had the right solution. "And, I will tell him how angry I am about them not telling me. Yeah, that's what I'll do. Let it all out. We have never hidden our feelings from each other. It's better that way." With a plan of action decided, he went into the master berth and flung himself face down onto the bed.

The rising sun produced a warmth that kept Drew sound asleep, until a haunting melody rang in his head:

> *I could have my Gucci on*
> *I could wear my Louis Vuitton*
> *But even with nothin' on*
> *Bet I made you look, I made you look*
> *Ooh*
> *When I walk, walk*

Over and over the words of Megan Trainor's song *I Made You Look* repeated in Drew's head. It was Drew's special ring tone.

"My phone, my cell phone." Drew, still in a deep fog, reached for the phone on the headboard behind him only to knock it to the floor. He rolled onto his side, looked down, and pushed the speaker button on the phone.

"Hello . . . hello," he said in a faint raspy voice.

"Drew you all right? You safe?"

"Yeah. Pat?"

"Where are you?"

` "At the boat. What's wrong?"

"Nothing. I went by the loft and you weren't in."

"What time is it?"

"Nine-sixteen," Pat replied.

Drew sat upright, rubbing both eyes. "Hey, man, since you're up, do you want to come by? We need to talk."

"Sure," Pat replied. "Be at the marina in thirty minutes."

Drew got up, looked about. He reached down and picked up his boxer briefs from the floor. He pulled them up and looked for his pants.

*Oh, yeah, they're on the floor by the galley sink.* He went into the main cabin, put on his pants, and went back into the master stateroom. He opened a locker door and chose a T-shirt with the scene of a surfer thrashing a wave on the back. As he returned to the main cabin, his mind began racing.

*Okay, Drew, be matter a fact when Pat arrives. Don't loose your cool. Just ask why everyone didn't tell me my father was still alive. Yeah, that's it.*

He sat at the table again, nervous as ever. Time passed slowly as he waited. Then, a familiar voice.

"Permission to come aboard."

"Come," was all he could say. *That was dumb. I can't let him know how upset I am. Be cool. Think before you talk.*

Pat emerged as he stepped down the ladder to the main cabin. He took one look at Drew and said, "Son, what's wrong?"

"Ah, have a seat," Drew replied as he pointed to the bench across from the cabin table where he was seated.

"You've been threatened?"

"Pat . . ."

"Yes, Drew?"

"Why didn't you tell me my father was still alive," Drew blurted out.

Pat sat back against the bench cushions. "So, you know. Who told you?"

"The Feds. But I need you to tell me why you and Lauren said my father was dead. Died in a car crash."

"What are you doing talking to the Feds? It was the FBI, right?"

"Pat, please, just tell me why the lie." The pain of having to ask obvious in his voice.

"We wanted to tell you dozens of times, but your mother said no. She made us swear not to. She thought it best. When she passed, Lauren and I decided you had to know but we could never find the right time. As you became a man, we just couldn't do it."

"Mom said you couldn't tell me, why?"

The investigator paused. He looked at Drew and in a controlled tone said, "The guy's a shithead. At first he denied paternity until your mom got a DNA test. Then he refused to pay child support. They fought constantly. Finally, she had enough. Your mother drew up a contract waiving child support but only if the man promised to stay out of your life."

"Pat, a mother can't waive a child's right for financial support from the father. No court would honor such an agreement."

"She knew that. So when he refused, she blackmailed him with all sorts of photographs and even a video of him with prostitutes."

"How did she get those?"

"She had me follow him."

"Man he is a fucked dude," Drew said as he began to realize how his father had treated his mother.

"Your mother promised not to reveal what I found if he never got involved with you. He agreed."

"That's it. He decided to disown me for that?"

"Yes. What you don't know is he is into very deviant sex. Sadomasochism, master-servant role playing. You name it, he has done it."

"Did that asshole do those things to my mother?"

"No. It was a onetime affair with him. Just at the wrong time of the month for her."

"Did he force himself on her?"

"That is how he is. The man takes what he wants. When he was a younger man, it was a common practice for him. He never took no for an answer. He called her into his chambers and locked the door. Your mother felt it best not to make a scene. So she gave in that one time rather than have him take revenge as he was known to do."

"That's no excuse."

"Drew, the man was her boss. She was a new court reporter and needed the job."

"The Feds told me a judge was in cahoots with Mayfield and Mayor Sandleson. But they never said his name. Only that he was my father. So who is he?"

"They didn't say who he was?"

Drew just looked at his investigator and waited.

"All right, you have a right to know. He is Judge Brian O'Shea."

"No, Pat. No. It can't be true."

"Sorry, Drew, but he's your father."

Drew, emotionally overwhelmed leaned back and looked down into his lap. The news was more than he had expected. Finally, he asked, "How many times Pat? How many? He just couldn't have done it . . ."

Pat interrupted. He could see the pain on the young man's face. "Only once, Drew. She immediately transferred out of his department. Everyone knew how O'Shea was, so the head court clerk quickly reassigned her to a judge in an outlying courthouse."

"I can see why Mom didn't want me to know."

"There's more. When she was dying, your mother told me to duplicate the evidence I had on Brian and send copies to two out-of-state attorneys. I was to threaten O'Shea." Pat paused a moment, before continuing. "Let's just say I was to intervene if he started to come around or tried to get involved in your life. Several times I had to remind Brian I had copies of the contract and all the evidence."

"Has he done so recently?"

"Yes, numerous times after your mother passed."

"Pat, that's blackmail."

"No. I just reminded him she had instructed two out-of-state attorneys to release the documents to the news media if he tried anything. She especially wanted me to tell him the video and pictures would be included."

"Oh, that's rich. He must have blown a gasket."

"Gasket hell. Worse than that. Remember, it is the messenger not the message the king takes revenge on."

"My mother was quite a fighter."

"You were her whole life, Drew. She never got serious with another man. Her constant concern was about you—protecting you was her obsession. As she got weaker, her only thought was keeping O'Shea away from you." Pat started to say more but hesitated. A long silence followed.

Finally, Drew spoke. "Pat, thank you. I understand. Mom, Lauren, and you were doing what was best for me. You are right, I wouldn't have understood any of this if you had told me about O'Shea when I was younger. Only now that I've seen how he tries to manipulate my practice, my life, hell even my sex life, do I fully understand what kind of a devious, controlling dick he is."

"Your sex life"?"

"Yeah. He set me up with Judge Judith Hudson."

Oh, that one. I didn't know. Any others?"

"Hell, I don't know. When I told him to stay out of my life that's when he told me about Judith. He even said he's been sending me all sorts of clients. When I cursed his meddling, he chastised me for being an ungrateful son. I thought he was referring to my age. I didn't know at the time he really meant I was his son."

"Drew, I didn't know about all this. Sorry. If I had known, I would have stopped it."

"No, Pat. It's best I handle him on my own."

"I'm . . . we are . . ." Pat muttered haltingly. "Lauren and I were very worried how you would . . ."

Seeing Pat's regret about not saying anything, Drew said, "You did it out of love. That's all I needed to know."

More silence followed as the two tried to understand what just happened. Finally, Pat tried to change the subject.

"Ah, Drew, I don't want to make light about what Lauren and I did, but I have to ask, why were you talking to the FBI?"

"Oliver Wyland lured me to his office so he could get me and you to help him arrest corrupt San Diego officials. They think O'Shea and some other officials are part of a big kickback scheme involving the mayor, the mayor's political advisor, the police chief, and a guy named Morgan Mayfield."

"The chief and Mayfield? What's that got to do with you, Drew?" Pat paused. Oh, wait a minute. They said you and me."

"That's right. Wyland thinks the Guerra case ties Detective Clayton and Chief Shaughnessy to the city's corrupt officials.

Oly says Shaughnessy is part of the corrupt city scheme. Mancini said they hide their money in the Caribbean."

"I see."

"Wait, there's more. Oly specifically named Mayfield and the mayor, who has to be Sam Sandleson, as owners of those corporate bank accounts. And Mancini told me the FBI has a copy of all those bank records. Pat, that's got to be the Cayman Island accounts you uncovered."

"Drew, I think the FBI is talking about something big, probably some sort of embezzlement or theft.

"Yup, and Mayfield is the guy they use to launder the money," surmised Hawke. "The way Wyland and Mancini explained it, the mayor greases Mayfield's projects through city hall using a judge and Chief Shaughnessy whenever problems come up."

"When did they tell you all this?"

"Actually, they really didn't tell me about O'Shea. They just kept saying judges were involved along with my father. It was you who said my father was O'Shea, the Presiding Judge of the Superior Courts. That was enough for me to put two and two together."

"What specifically does Wyland want from us?"

"He's got this plan to lure Clayton into making incriminating statements to you. From there they intend to coerce Clayton or Shaughnessy into telling them how this gang of five operates."

"Drew, I think you left out the key words . . . 'use us.' "

"What do you mean?"

"As I hear you, Wyland wants to record me baiting Clayton into making incriminating statements about the murder of Juan De Jesus."

Drew started to say something, but Pat raised his hand. "Why should we get involved in all this?"

Drew didn't say anything. Pat waited. Finally his investigator asked, "Drew, why did you go to see Wyland?"

Drew's eyes watered up. He cleared his throat but said nothing.

"Son, tell me, why see the Man?"

With his voice cracking, he said, "Because I didn't want you killed."

"By who? You mean Clayton and the other officers?"

"Yes. I was afraid for you, Lauren, and possibly Debbie. Mancini said you all could be in danger. I didn't want to lose the ones I love. So I called Finnigan, the CIA agent."

Pat interrupted. "The agent that wanted to use you in the Pansky case?"

"He gave me this battery extender for my phone. It turns my phone into a secure line where I can call him. I felt I could ask him what to do. He told me we had to talk over a secure line at Wyland's office. So I went there. When I got there, Wyland told me he was the one who could help everyone."

"You don't have to say anything more. That's when they told you about the corruption in city government."

"Yes, but I still refused their help. So Wyland told me my biological father was one of the officials involved in the corruption."

"Drew, the Feds are just using us for their own purposes. We are pawns in their plan to end this government corruption."

"I know, but how else could I make sure the Enforcers don't kill you? The FBI has an entire team of agents assembled to carry out their plan. They began protecting you even before Lauren flew to Colorado. She and her sister are now being protected by agents outside her sister's house and they are followed wherever they go."

"Drew, we are dealing with rogue cops. They can pick out a tail or another officer guarding a home or protecting someone in an instant. If they see the Feds guarding you and me, it will tip them off. There's only one conclusion the bad cops can come to . . . I've turned informant. That would sign our death warrants."

"God, Pat, I didn't mean to. What are we to do? We better tell Lauren, and I'll tell Wyland no deal." Drew started to get up only to have Pat rise and say no.

"But, Pat, you said . . ."

"Sit down. Let's think this through." Drew slowly sat back into his seat as Pat continued. "Wyland and company want to use us to catch a bunch of crooks. The Enforcers want to shut me up one way or another. Seems to me there must be a way we can use these two cross purposes for our own needs."

# CHAPTER TWELVE

**Tuesday, 7:20 a.m.**

Drew sat in his office, thinking about the coming meeting. His right hand aimlessly turned the pages of the Guerra file as he thought about what he had gotten everyone into. Always the thought of Pat being killed or even Guerra, just like Manny, repeatedly interrupted his thoughts.

*I had no choice. I had to go to them for Pat and Guerra's sake. Now everything is all screwed up.*

Suddenly, a noise came from the office hallway. He glared at his office door. Slowly, it opened. Drew stood, his leg pushing back the desk chair, waiting to see who might be coming in.

"Drew, good morning. What are you doing here so early?" greeted Debbie McCaleb with a smile.

"Nothing, Debbie."

"You don't look it," came the reply as the hefty woman observed Drew's tense expression.

"Debbie, I called Pat, Liz, and Matt. They will be here shortly after eight to discuss the Guerra case. Buzz me when they arrive."

"Andrew Jackson Hawke, I knows when you're upset. Now what's wrong?"

"Debbie, please, the meeting is about what we're going to do with Guerra."

"Humph," came the reply. "Don't lie to me. I knows when something bad has happened to you."

"Debbie, it's nothing. Guerra is just a problem, that's all. Now please get the conference room ready and buzz me when everyone is ready."

She turned and walked off, "You know, Andrew, you're a *bad* liar."

A few moments later, the office door opened and in walked three men dressed in white overalls and carrying equipment.

"A.J. Hawke, is he in?"

"And who might you be?" demanded the protective black woman as she rose from her desk to confront the men.

"Tell Mr. Hawke we are here to do our electronic security sweep."

Just then Drew emerged from his office. "That's okay, Debbie. They're with the FBI."

The woman turned. "Andrew Jackson, what in the world is going on?"

"Debbie, everything will be explained at the meeting this morning. Let them do their job." At that moment, FBI Agent Kiefer Mancini walked in.

"Debbie, this is Kiefer Mancini, he will be part of our meeting this morning. Please let me know when Pat, Liz, and Matt get in. Oh, you are to attend also."

Debbie stood there with her mouth open as the three FBI technicians went about setting up their equipment.

"Ma'am," the smaller of the men asked politely, "I'll have to ask you to move so I can work on your phone system."

"Oh no you don't. This is my desk and you isn't touching anything," came the reply.

"Debbie, let them do their job," Drew said in a raised voice as he and Mancini walked into his office and shut the door.

"Well, I declare," she exclaimed in an exasperated tone. Still refusing to move, the man asked again politely, "I'll only be a few minutes, ma'am, may I?"

"Oh, all right. But don't you dare mess with my papers. They's important," she demanded.

Debbie reluctantly stepped aside. Standing, she looked around bewildered as her orderly office was being swarmed by technicians with strange equipment looking for audio and video surveillance devices. A fourth man walked in with a tall ladder and began removing the office ceiling tiles. With a saddened expression on her face, she turned and walked out into the hallway and to the only place she knew for privacy, the women's bathroom.

When Debbie finally returned, Liz and Matt were standing at the office door.

"Debbie, what's going on?" asked Liz.

"I don't know, but Drew shouldn't keep us in the dark. How can we protect him if he acts like this?"

As Liz, Debbie, and Matt talked, Pat De Luca came down the hallway.

"Hey, guys, what's happening?"

"Debbie says it's the FBI," offered Matt.

"Oh, no," came Pat with a surprised expression.

Another man, slight in build, wearing black trousers, a peach-colored shirt, and a tweed sports jacket exited the elevator and approached.

Debbie stepped slightly in front of the doorway as he got close. "May I help you?"

"I'm with the FBI; I have an eight o'clock meeting. I'm Doctor F. Simon Powell," he added, seeing the puzzled look on her face.

"Let him go, Debbie, I think I know what Drew has done," Pat said in a somewhat sad voice.

Once Dr. Powell stepped inside, he looked back. "Has agent Mancini arrived yet?"

"Yes," answered Debbie, pointing to the closed door. "He's in Drew's office."

ooooo

At 8:30 a.m., everyone gathered in the conference room. "Thank you for coming early, especially you, Matt," Drew said. "I know I'm imposing on your busy class schedule, but what you are about to hear is very important."

He gestured to the end of the conference table. "You may remember FBI agent Kiefer Mancini from the Pansky murder case. To his right is Dr. F. Simon Powell, who also works for the FBI. Dr. Powell is a specialist in police behavioral analysis. Gentlemen, this is my staff. To my right is Ms. Debra McCaleb, my office manager, to her right is my private investigator, Patrick De Luca. To my left is Ms. Elizabeth Bernquist, my associate attorney, and to her left is my office file clerk and general gofer man, Mathew Van Dryden."

Looking back to Kiefer, he said, "Agent Mancini, please go from here."

"Thank you. I have admired from afar your team efforts in support of Mr. Hawke. It is because of you, he approached us. Unbeknownst to Drew, we have been investigating certain San Diego officials for several years. When he told us about the Guerra case and the threat against Mr. De Luca, it became apparent the corruption we want to end somehow involves the San Diego police officers who are threatening Mr. De Luca."

To everyone's surprise, Matt spoke up. "What corruption are you talking about?"

Drew started to respond, then caught himself. *No, Matt*

*has a right to ask all the questions he wants. He, too, could be in danger.*

Mancini paused. "Good question. I wasn't planning on going into such detail, but Drew did tell us his staff had a right to know why we are here and how you could be affected."

Mancini stood up and continued. "What I am about to tell you must be kept secret. Otherwise, you risk the lives of everyone in this room."

The agent's last words caused Debbie, Liz, and Matt to look at each other.

"Mr. Van Dryden the Third . . ." Matt appeared surprised the agent knew his full name. ". . . that means you can't discuss any of this with your college friends or even your prominent mother and father, whom I'm sure would demand to know all the details."

"You know about my parents?"

"The FBI doesn't work with anyone unless we know them and their background. In this case, it's very important we know who's involved and how we must protect all of you."

"Protect us? Protect me?" asked the startled college student.

"Yes, Mr. Van Dryden. The people who are making threats against Mr. De Luca are part of a gang of officers you know as the Enforcers. We, however, think some or all of them are tied to corrupt city government officials. So, to put it bluntly, if they feel it necessary to threaten Mr. De Luca, the FBI believes they could do the same to Drew and to you three."

Liz looked at Drew with a concerned look, "Sir, you feel Drew is at risk because they threatened Pat?"

"Yes. The best way to insure someone's silence is to kill them or in your case to probably threaten those who just might know too much. As part of Mr. Hawke's law firm, you are therefore also at risk. Drew told us Mr. De Luca and you are his family. That is especially true about you, Mrs. McCaleb. All of you being close to Drew could be in danger as they try to keep Mr. De Luca and Mr. Hawke silent."

Debbie's reaction was one of disgust. "I told you, Andrew Hawke, this Guerra matter is no good. Yes, no good! I told you we should not take it. Um-hmm," she admonished, shaking her head, "bad blood all the way around."

Drew started to reply but Mancini continued.

"Mrs. McCaleb, it's not your attorney's fault. He was doing what any good attorney should do, think of his client and realize the twenty-year-old murder charges were wrong. What he didn't know was that those charges are part of a plan to silence Mr. Guerra until they can arrange for his death while he's in prison. A fate we believe these crooks arranged for Manny De Jesus."

Matt again spoke. "Why should they want to kill Carlos Guerra now, and, for that matter, threaten Pat after so many years? I mean, Mr. Guerra has been out of prison for fifteen, sixteen years."

"Past crimes have a way of coming back to haunt perpetrators. In this case, those involved in the murder of Juan and Manny De Jesus. These men are now in very important positions in the police department. A scandal could end their careers. And Drew Hawke is just the type of attorney who could uncover the murders. Not yet understood is how Officer Clayton is tied to San Diego's corrupt government officials."

Liz raised her hand.

"Yes, Ms. Bernquist?"

"If you don't know whether the officer who killed Juan De Jesus is part of the corruption you are investigating, why come to us?"

"One of the other police officers involved in the coverup of the murder of Juan De Jesus is now one of the five officials we believe are using their offices in a kickback scheme to the tune of millions of dollars, which they have secreted offshore. I'm sure these officials don't want some stupid act committed decades ago by a member of their inner circle to somehow expose their criminal enterprise."

Pat De Luca asked, "You're referring to the money in the Cayman Islands?"

"Yes, sir."

"Oh, my goodness, Drew, what are we going to do? That is the SMA Construction case."

"Yes, Mrs. McCaleb," responded Mancini. "Through another client, you have stumbled onto how the gang of five have been hiding their money offshore. Now you see how all the pieces fit together and why you are potential targets."

Drew looked at his friends as they realized the full extent of the mess they were in. *I'm so sorry guys*, was his only thought.

"If I may, folks, I want to get to the immediate problems at hand." Mancini retook his seat and opened a small folder. "First, we have swept your office for listening and video devices. It is clean."

Matt again spoke up. "Why are you looking for surveillance devices?"

"We are dealing with suspects who are police officers, officers who have access to the latest monitoring equipment. We had to make sure they couldn't listen in on what we tell you. In fact, the four technicians in the other room have an electronic shield up to prevent anyone in a nearby building from listening."

The tension in the room became palpable as Mancini revealed the sophisticated measures being taken. "We are now installing video surveillance cameras, which will monitor twenty-four seven what happens in this office. Tomorrow, one of our agents will join you as a new employee. She has a law degree, has worked in a law firm, and is one of our most experienced field agents."

"You said she. What am I to do with her?" asked Debbie. "Everything is handled. We really don't need another person."

"Our agent is expertly trained and knows how to protect you and herself. She will be in the office as long as it is open. This way, you have protection close at hand as well as by the agents next door and in the building across the way. Whenever you leave the office, you will be followed. At night, your residence will be under surveillance by two agents."

"Cool," commented Matt.

"You, Mr. Van Dryden, are a problem."

The young man looked startled. "I don't understand. I won't say anything."

"You have classes amongst hundreds of students and are in constant motion. This doesn't even consider the difficulty of protecting you if you go out or run to Taco Bell for a late-night snack."

"How'd you know I love Taco Bell?"

"You all have been under surveillance since we first learned of the threat."

Pat started to say something but Mancini continued.

"Yes, Mr. De Luca, we have been outside your house since Friday night, and your wife is currently being protected by agents out of our Denver office. Lauren is safe."

"Is my wife still with her sister?"

"Yes. That was a very good idea to send her out of harm's way."

Looking about, the agent asked, "Do you have any more questions about your protection and who will be doing it?"

Matt raised his hand.

"Yes, Matt. May I call you Matt?"

"Of course. Do I have a female agent following me too?"

"You will never know who follows you. Just don't sneak out or try to avoid our protection. We don't care if you smoke pot or do something stupid. We're here to protect you. So, when you go out, don't be sneaky. Stay in the open and be casual. Well, actually, just be normal in your movements. Above all don't look around to see if we are following."

"Yes, sir. So I can be and do what I usually do?"

"Absolutely. Now I would like Dr. Powell to explain why we think you are in such danger. Dr. Powell?"

"Thank you, Kiefer." Powell stood and cleared his throat.

"The people we are dealing with are not only dangerous, but they are also not stupid. These are police officers who have taken justice into their own hands. Do not forget, the police deal with the dregs of society. They are constantly surrounded by violence. Police are the lid that keeps society's violence under control." Powell cleared his throat again.

"Regrettably, many officers come to believe the only way they can survive is through acts of violence and intimidation. For such officers, their first reaction is to use force, even to kill. In many respects they live and die by the gun. Accordingly, we must expect the worst from this rogue gang of officers.

"Since these men know every aspect of policing, they also know how to conduct surveillance. As such, they know when someone is being protected. Therefore, the FBI must take every precaution possible in our investigation and in the task of protecting you. Our job is extremely difficult because our suspects have access to every modern means of police tactics. They can easily figure out we are involved and how we protect you. Thus, to do this successfully, you must cooperate one hundred percent. Otherwise, you will be vulnerable, and the FBI may even fail to capture these criminals.

"Now, knowing these are very skilled and experienced officers, we believe they know killing someone at this stage of their cover up is foolish. It would just raise too many red flags. For that reason, the FBI is proceeding on two tracks. First, to provide protection for you as Agent Mancini outlined. Caution is our primary goal.

"Second, the FBI assumes these officers will first try to intimidate rather than kill. To this end, all of your office and personal communications are now being listened to and all your actions are being observed in case they try to contact you."

Mancini could see no one liked such personal intrusion, so he interrupted. "Please understand, all of you are potential victims. If they want to silence Mr. De Luca, Drew is the obvious one to go after. To silence Drew, they threaten Pat and, of course, one of you. What better way to drive home their demand for silence than to arrange an accidental death for one of you."

Undeterred by the blunt warning, Liz asked, "Drew, our clients expect attorney-client privilege. Aren't we violating that duty and the constitutional right to private counsel by letting the FBI listen to what we do, and, worse yet, what the clients tell us?"

Agent Mr. Mancini answered. "Every step will be taken to protect the right to an attorney and the privacy of attorney-client communications. Our embedded agent will view no case files or sit in on any client meetings nor listen to any phone calls between you and your clients. A computer analyses each conversation by listening for key words. If any statement or conversation implies a threat or relates to any of our suspects and what they do, our supervising agents will be alerted to listen."

Liz persisted. "You record all video and audio conversations?"

"The computer stores everything for seventy-two hours and erases them unless it detects something relevant to your safety or this case."

Both Liz and Debbie still looked concerned.

Mancini tried again. "How about this. I will arrange for you and Drew to visit our communications center and have the technicians fully explain how we intend to surveil all communications. We will also provide you with a copy of the federal court order outlining how we must proceed when protecting attorneys and their clients' constitutional privileges. Please understand, your protection is vital to the FBI's plan to capture this gang. In doing so, we take every step possible not to violate your clients' rights."

"And how do you plan to get these bastards," asked Debbie in the most unladylike manner.

"That we can't tell you, but the plan is already underway," came agent Mancini's curt reply. "If you don't have any further questions for Dr. Powell or about our plan to protect you, I would like . . ."

Matt raised his hand.

"Yes, Matt?"

"I have a question for Dr. Powell. May I?"

"Yes, of course."

"Doctor, I have a friend who wants to be a police officer. His father and grandfather were cops. Can you tell me why he might go bad. He thinks all cops are heroes. He wants to fight crime and be a good one."

Drew started to rise and say something, but Dr. Powell looked at Drew and shook his head. "Great question. One that needs to be answered. Simply put, it is the human phenomenon of 'Them versus Us.' By nature, human beings want to belong. We are a tribal people who take care of one another. That is how the individual survives. To that end, we bond with those that we have a strong sense of shared values, meaning, or purpose. Many times that bond arises out of fear or danger. To protect that bond, people will fight and die for each other."

"You mean like in war?"

"Yes, Matt. Woodrow Wilson described our entry into World War I as a war to make the world 'safe for democracy.' This call rallied a nation to war. Roosevelt similarly unified this nation when attacked at Pearl Harbor."

"But, sir, how does that apply to police officers killing unarmed people?'

"Police officers are charged with protecting society. But, Matt, some lawbreakers resist, even fight back or kill."

"You mean like the punks that killed two officers while they were parked in their car?"

"Yes. In some neighborhoods, it is open warfare between groups of criminals protecting their illegal ways of making money and the police trying to eliminate prostitution, robbery, extortion, drugs, and other acts of human degradation."

"I see."

"To combat this, the police rely on their tribe of fellow officers to protect one another, even come to their aid when lawbreakers fight back. Some officers view certain groups of people as scum, even inferior. As a result such officers treat those lives as being less valuable than the ones they try to protect. Such ways of thinking allows some officers to violently abuse suspects. It also makes it easier to shoot first, even when they are not sure the suspect is armed. In very violent neighborhoods, officers become both judge, jury, and executioner as they use violence to invoke fear in order to maintain order and protect one another. We believe this is what happened to the De Jesus brothers."

"But, sir, what about minority officers abusing their own kind?"

"Okay, Matt, I think that's enough," Drew said as he started to rise.

"Actually, Mr. Hawke, may I answer his question?"

Drew settled back into his chair.

"Thank you, sir." Looking directly at the young college student, Dr. Powell said, "Matt sometimes minority officers are harsher on their own than their white counterparts. This comes from anger not just because of the criminal act itself, but also because of the shame it reflects on their race and the need to show allegiance with the other officers."

Pat De Luca spoke up. "Matt, the problem is, officers rely on one another to survive. The need to have officers coming to your aid leads some not to report the criminal acts of fellow officers."

"What we are trying to say, folks," Mancini forcibly injected, "is that such wrong thinking leads to the existence of groups, cliques, whatever you want to call them, within police departments. We even find such groups within special crime units formed to suppress crime waves. In other instances, actual police gangs form, like the Enforcers, a gang similar to the Banditos, the Grim Reapers, Vikings, and the Executioners that have existed for decades or do currently exist within the Los Angeles Sheriff's Department. Gangs where the deputies have their own initiation rites, body tattoos, and rules on how offenders are treated."

Such an admission shocked Drew and his staff, further underlining the seriousness of their situation.

"Now," Mancini added as he stood, "I would like to meet with Mr. De Luca and Drew, alone."

Matt seemed unsatisfied as he looked to Drew and then to Debbie. Debbie, not accustomed to being left out of things, nor the agent's dismissive tone, rose.

"It appears we are not wanted any further. Let's give these boys their privacy," the woman said in a somewhat sarcastic tone as she gestured for Matt and Elizabeth to follow her.

As the three left the conference room, she suggested, "Why don't we go downstairs and get a cup of coffee."

# CHAPTER THIRTEEN

**Tuesday, 4:10 p.m.**

It had been a difficult day. No one had talked to anyone else. At least not to Drew, who sequestered alone in his office with his own thoughts. The others grew silent every time Drew emerged from his office, heads buried in files or glued to a computer screen. The young lawyer's isolation was clearly written across his face as he walked out of the office without saying a word to his loyal staff that neither acknowledged his leaving nor appeared to care.

*Man, these guys must think I'm an ogre for wanting to fire them. They must know I'm thinking only of their safety. God, don't they know I love them?*

Drew felt lost. Until these bizarre events, he only had to think of himself, how to protect himself in a violent world, how to release the tension of being young by drinking, raising hell, and having sex with anyone he wanted and as many times as he felt like it. It was a freedom he no longer had. He had begun to realize everything he did from here on out could endanger those he valued most. Not just Pat and Lauren, but Debbie, Liz, and Matt.

*I just don't know what to do. Fuck, man, this hurts.*

Drew exited through the Keating's gold-trimmed glass doors onto F Street, turned left, and headed toward the Ace parking lot across 5th Avenue. As he entered the parking garage, he said out loud, "Mario and Julian had better come up with some good ideas."

"Hey, Jefe, wassup?" Mario greeted as he extended a high five and the two did their thing.

But Drew was not enthusiastic. "You're exceedingly happy, Mario. Tell me you got good news."

"This way to my detailing house of magic," Mario replied, pointing to the large shade canopy. Once there, Julian greeted Drew with a big smile and a strong hand shake.

"Let me turn on this high-frequency sound jammer," the computer wizard said. "There, now we can talk, but softly."

"What is that?" asked Drew in a hushed voice.

"It blocks laser microphone snooping. The cops use these directional lasers to listen in on conversations from hundreds of feet away. So we have to whisper. Some of the latest equipment is extremely sensitive."

Drew nodded.

"Here's what I found on your BMW." Julian directed Drew over to the Beamer. "See here?" He pointed to a factory OBT2 port under the Beamer's dash.

"You mean next to the fuse box?"

"Yeah, but here," Julian said, waving his index finger over a small black object plugged into the port.

"I see it. What is it?"

"It's a device I designed to monitor the car's GPS tracking system. My device collects the car's active and passive GPS information. When the car transmits such information via cellular or satellite networks to a GPS host computer center, which by the way the FBI can monitor, my device allows me access to the same information."

"Isn't that illegal?"

"Let's not worry about that."

"Oh-kay," Drew slowly remarked. "Ah, Julian, are you saying the government can track my car?"

"They indeed do."

"Oh, shit! The FBI has been following my movements!"

"Yes. Actually, there's a lot more. The FBI currently monitors the homes of your individual employees and Pat De Luca through their home and personal computers. Remember how I found your computer was being monitored? They've done the same to your friends' computers, and they have established camera surveillance as well. FBI agents are also monitoring your friends' homes using directional parabolic and laser microphones and infrared equipment as part of the protection you requested for you friends."

"Julian, can you hack into—"

"Yes, I already have. I currently can see and hear what the FBI does."

"How in the world did you do that?"

"It's a long explanation and you probably don't want to know. In any event, remember I used to develop and monitor programs for that purpose as well as anti-hacking programs to protect FBI surveillance."

"Simply diabolical, Julian. I didn't know you knew how do to such things."

"This is what I did when I was with the CIA and the FBI. I created such programs."

Drew looked at the man with amazement. "So, my Tami program is just child's play to you?"

"It's a good program, Drew, but I think a high school kid could hack it. Not to fear, I will install a sophisticated program that will block any outside surveillance. Well, almost any."

"Then my loft will be safe?"

"Yes, somewhat. My program will alert any intrusion or disabling of my anti-hacking program, and it will automatically shut down Tami until the hacker reactivates her. But I will be alerted to what's happening. Now, we've been sidetracked. Back to GPS tracking. I also installed my device in Pat's car and those of your staff."

"So that's why you wanted me to keep them in the office as long as possible."

"Yes, the timing was perfect."

"Julian, I'm impressed with what you've done, but how do we keep the Feds from knowing you hacked their programs?"

"Well, that is a problem. It probably will take them many hours since I hid my code amongst theirs. They have to somehow be alerted it exists in order for them to specifically look for it, and, even then, I routed my copy of the signal through various servers throughout the world. It'll take them a couple of days or more. By then I will know they found it and can redirect the signal through a whole new set of servers."

"You are clever, Julian."

"See, Jefe? I told you Julian was good," Hawke's longtime friend added with a smile.

"It's not fool proof, Mr. Hawke. Sooner or later they will get to me, especially if their systems self-examine themselves, which they should. But I will be alerted as soon as they lock onto my programs. By the time the Feds go through all the servers, all they will find is an abandoned computer in some garage. We should be good for a few days, maybe a week, at the outside two weeks. Hopefully, I will have a new way to surveil everyone by then."

"How do you know it will work? Have you tested the program?"

"Yes, I've viewed the homes of your staff through the FBI

surveillance system. And I have been following De Luca's car for a little over an hour."

"What do you have to do next?"

"I just need to enter the VIN number of each remaining car, their license plate numbers, and color of vehicles into my computer. Mario got that info for me."

"Sí, Jefe."

"Next, I have to set up an AI central monitoring system, which will alert you, Mario, and myself whenever the FBI surveillance system detects a suspicious activity at their homes, your office, or when your friends are on the move."

"How long will all that take?"

"Hours, Drew, hours of computer time. I'll be busy most of tonight. But the AI generating programs I have will greatly speed things up."

"I have one more question. Will your surveillance program work with Matt, my file clerk? He's in college."

"Matt is a problem," Julian acknowledged. "I expect there will be all sorts of false alarms caused by people going in and out of his apartment. My AI program won't be able to differentiate between a college friend or a potential threat. We have to rely on the federal agents following Matt for real-time protection."

"Drew, why don't you get a drink at the Tipsy Crow and I'll finish registering the Beamer and your friends' cars for my GPS monitoring program. Then I'll go home and set up the twenty-four-hour AI monitoring center."

"You're convinced the AI surveillance center will alert us all?"

"Yes. The program will notify you and Mario automatically through home and laptop computers. Even your Apple watch will beep an alert."

"You and Julian are, well, I don't know how to say it . . . just great. You promised a twenty-four seven surveillance of my friends and you've done it. Thank you."

"I appreciate that, Drew. But remember, we will not be able to get to your friends to protect them. We're just able to surveil and monitor them. You really are counting on the FBI to provide onsite protection."

"I understand, Julian."

"And, Drew, as I said at the loft, we still might be able to provide close protection if the FBI does in fact plan to use Pat as bait."

"I know. The big problem is Pat, and the Feds are excluding me from their plans."

"Drew, our monitoring system may yet tell us what that plan is."

"Don't worry, Jefe. My people and I are ready to go on moment's notice. We with you."

"Mario, do you want to join me for a drink?"

"No, man. Can't. I'm on duty till two-thirty a.m."

Twenty minutes later, to Drew's surprise, Debbie, Liz, and Matt found their boss upstairs in the Tipsy Crow lounge, sipping a relaxing whisky.

"Drew, may we join you?" Debbie asked.

Drew immediately stood. "Yes, of course." He gestured to the chairs next to the couch.

"Drew, we're sorry if we seemed a little hostile to you today."

"How'd you know I was here?"

"Mario told us when we saw your car was still in the lot," she replied.

"Guys, I'm not angry with you. I'm just worried sick about you. I've caused this mess, and I just don't know what to do to fix it. Letting you go seemed the safest way to protect you."

Everyone started to talk at the same time, but Debbie

shushed the two with her forceful statement, "We are not wilting flowers, Drew."

"Right on," added Matt.

"Drew, you know we love you and won't abandon you, no matter what you say," added Liz with an emotional crack to her voice.

"And another thing, Andrew Jackson," Debbie added. "I am not going anywhere no matter what you say. Now, how do I get a drink in this place?"

Drew was flabbergasted. "Debbie, you don't drink."

"I iz tonight."

"Oh-kay. I'll go down stairs and order. What's your poison?"

"Oh, no you don't, Andrew Jackson Hawke. I knows you. You'll come back up with some Shirly Temple thingy like you always do. Matt, I will have a rye whisky. Tell that handsome gray-hair bartender down there I want a Ward 8 with orange juice and grenadine. Light on the orange juice."

"Debbie!"

"Don't Debbie me, Andrew Jackson. I knows how you drink so don't call the kettle black."

"What?" Drew exclaimed.

Matt intervened. "Drew, the phrase is 'the pot calling the kettle black.' In other words, boss, don't be a hypocrite and criticize her for having a drink."

"Matt, that's enough. I know exactly what she meant. What is this, beat up on Drew night? I—"

Liz spoke up. "Drew, we just want to have fun. Let us do so with the guy we love and admire."

"Now that that is settled, what do you want, Liz?" asked Matt.

"Ask Jack if he has San Diego Brewing Company's Kombucha. If not, then a glass of Napa Valley Cabernet Sauvignon."

"Now that is more reasonable, Liz," replied Drew. "And, Matt, tell Jack to put it on my tab."

"My drink, too? I've got my ID."

"I don't need to know about your supposed new driver's license, Matt. But, yes, whatever you want."

# CHAPTER FOURTEEN

**Two weeks later**

Matt was having a ball driving the BMW convertible as he took Drew and Liz the long way to court for Carlos Guerra's Friday morning special bail hearing. After each stop sign, their chauffeur would accelerate off the line as the light turned green, pressing Liz back against the rear seat.

"Drew, why don't you say something to Matt about his driving," complained Liz as she leaned forward so Drew could hear her complaints over the roar of the engine. "Isn't he going too fast?" she asked while trying to protect her hair from the wind.

"Relax, Liz, I got it all under control," replied Matt. "Right, Drew?"

Trying to keep truce in the family, Drew suggested, "Maybe a little bit slower, Matt, so we get to court without being stopped by the police."

Once in front of the courthouse, Drew stepped out and pushed the passenger front seat forward to let Liz out. As they walked up the courthouse steps, Liz continued to complain.

"Drew, why do you trust him to drive your car? No telling where he goes and what he does after dropping us off."

Drew wasn't listening. His thoughts were preoccupied with

how the DA and, for that matter, the judge would react to the dramatic events to come.

Drew looked at Liz. *Was it a mistake not to tell Liz what's going to happen? If she learns I knew about the federal action, she will be pissed I didn't tell her.*

Once through security, the two headed to Department 9. Inside, they were greeted by the court bailiff, Deputy Sheriff Tre Stout, who gestured for the two to come forward.

"Mr. Hawke, the judge will hear your case first."

"Call me Drew, Tre. I'm still the young lawyer in town."

"Yes, but a damn good one."

"Don't jinx me, Tre."

The two laughed as they entered the well of the court. Tre whispered, "The good-looking woman in the first row, that's Assistant U.S. Attorney Liberty Jala. The one right behind Assistant DA Farrat and Detective Clayton."

Drew and Elizabeth turned and looked. Trying to make light of Tre's comment, Drew said, "She looks like trouble."

Tre laughed. "You're always in trouble. That's what I like about you."

Once seated, Liz leaned close to Drew and asked, "What's a federal attorney doing here?" Before Drew could reply, Deputy Stout announced, "Hear ye, hear ye, this court is now in session. The Honorable Judge Richard J. Brown presiding."

The unpretentious judge waved his hand. "Have a seat, folks. We have a very crowded calendar to get to."

As the judge sat, he said, "Good morning, Mr. Hawke and Ms. Bernquist. Oh, yes," he added, peering over his reading glasses, "nice to see you again Assistant DA Jack Farrat and Chief Detective Thomas Clayton."

Before any could respond, the judge told his court clerk, "Mary, for the record, please call the Hawke matter."

"State of California versus Carlos Guerra-Lopez. Attorneys, please make your appearances."

Farrat rose. "For the people, Assistant District Attorney Jack Farrat."

Thereafter, Drew rose. "Ms. Elizabeth Bernquist and Andrew Hawke for the defendant, who is appearing by video from the County Jail."

The judge shuffled a few papers and, upon finding his tentative ruling, said, "Mr. Hawke, why should I dismiss this case?"

"Your Honor, I thought this was a bail hearing I requested due to the DA's failure to produce evidence about the carjacking."

"You're correct. However, I see the issues you raise in your dismissal motion are directly pertinent to my releasing Mr. Guerra on OR or bail."

"I see." Drew paused to collect his thoughts. Liz pulled the dismissal motion from her briefcase and shoved it in front of Drew.

The judge, seeing Hawke's delay, went on. "First, Mr. Hawke, I'm not particularly impressed with your argument that double jeopardy applies. Both our state Supreme Court and the federal Supreme Court have held murder is a separate crime that can be prosecuted even though the defendant has pled guilty to the underlying crime associated with the killing. Your comment."

"Sir, you are correct. However, Mr. Guerra was originally charged with killing Juan De Jesus under our felony murder rule as well as Penal Code section 215 (a), carjacking. In my opinion, the carjack is a necessary part of the homicide charge. You can't charge a co-conspirator under the felony-murder rule without the car theft. And, Your Honor, my client was originally charged with both the carjack and the homicide.

However, the then-DA offered, and my client accepted, a plea bargain to the lesser charge of carjacking. I submit he was offered such a plea because of his limited role in the car theft and that he wasn't present nor did he encourage De Jesus to shoot at the pursuing officer."

"If I understand correctly, you are saying once a plea bargain is finalized and the defendant is sentenced, the state is barred from further prosecution, even for the death of Juan De Jesus, because he was originally charged with murder." Judge Brown shook his head as if disagreeing.

Seeing the reaction, Drew quickly added, "Correct. And, Your Honor, any further prosecution, if allowed, should be done under the standards of Senate Bill 1437. Part of any decision to allow prosecution today should consider the circumstances of not only the car theft and the shooting, but also why the DA offered a plea deal to the carjack and not to murder."

Farrat immediately stood and interrupted. "Your Honor, the record should reflect that Manny De Jesus, a party to the carjack, was sentenced to life for the death of his brother Juan De Jesus."

"Mr. Farrat, you are correct, but I don't think that is the deciding issue on Mr. Hawke's motion to dismiss."

"Your Honor, may I continue?" Drew asked.

"Yes, please do, Mr. Hawke."

"The legislature mandated through 1437 that an accomplice cannot be prosecuted for a murder committed by a co-defendant unless the accomplice is a proactive participant in the planning and execution of the underlying felony or was a factor contributing to the actual killing."

Farrat was anxious to respond but the judge pointed for him sit down. "Let Mr. Hawke finish. You will have your time, Jack."

Turning back to Hawke, the judge said, "Yes, I read your motion. So the defense position is that Mr. Guerra can't be prosecuted twenty years later for the death of De Jesus because he was a minor participant in the carjack and had nothing to do with the shooting, correct?"

"Yes, sir."

"You also state in your papers, Mr. Hawke, that at this late date Mr. Guerra is prejudiced because all of the other participants in the carjack are now dead, and almost all of the police reports and physical evidence is missing. Is that correct?"

"Yes, Your Honor."

Farrat jumped to his feet again but a stern look from the judge caused him to sit back down.

"Your Honor," Drew pleaded, "I can't even tell which officers were involved in the car chase, witnessed the shooting, or how the apprehension of Mr. Guerra occurred. Further, any statements my client made to the police are missing. The police reports produced fail to state whether my client was a major or minor participant in the carjacking. How can I mount a defense under such circumstances?"

Looking to Farrat, the judge asked, "Jack, what do you say about this lack of evidence. Mr. Hawke calls it spoliation of evidence in his brief. I must say that is a rather condemning choice of words since spoilation can convey an illicit intent."

Finally being able to reply, the prosecutor rose. "Sir, the defendant should be prosecuted under the then-existing interruption of the felony-murder rule—"

"Even though," interrupted the judge, "the legislature says the standards of 1437 are retroactive to all defendants charged under the old rule?"

"Yes, sir. The actual language is 'sentenced and serving time,' not charged."

"Mr. Farrat, I find that a rather unique interpretation of the legislature's intent."

"Sir, the legislature discussed this very same issue. It would have been quite easy to craft language saying exactly what Mr. Hawke argues. But they didn't. The new legislation does not say 1437 standards apply to the prosecution of homicides committed prior to its passage. The people submit the legislature therefore intended the felony-murder rule existing at the time of the crime should be applied to any crime prosecuted in the future."

"I disagree, Mr. Farrat. There is lots of legal precedence clarifying the legislature's intent when a statute's language is later challenged. I also think the legislature's intent is quite clear here: the old application of the felony-murder rule was too expansive and unjust, violating many decades of legal interpretation of conspirator liability. Equally clear, 1437 mandates a new standard for prosecuting any accomplice under the felony murder rule. Don't you agree?"

"No, sir. The legislature specifically used language that specified which defendants 1437 should be retroactively applied to—those still serving time."

"Mr. Farrat, I agree 1437 specifically says the new accomplice language applies to convicts still incarcerated under the old felony-murder rule. But, I note, 1437 does not prohibit applying the new standards when prosecutors charge for old crimes. Don't you agree?"

"Well, yes, sir. However, the people submit the proper reading of the legislation is that prosecutors are not barred from using the then felony-murder rule in effect at the time of the crime, even though such prosecution doesn't occur until after 1437."

"And," Judge Brown forcibly added before Farrat could say

more, "the legislature emphatically found that prior felony-murder standards were onerous and unjust. I'm correct on that too. Do you agree, Jack?"

"Yes, sir. However, in all due respect, Your Honor, I think for any court to interrupt 1437 as Mr. Hawke wants is judicial legislation."

Drew immediately shot to his feet.

"Mr. Hawke, you are standing."

"Yes, sir. I wish to address the prosecutor's seeming blanket interpretation of my arguments."

"Proceed."

"Sir, since Marbury versus Madison in 1803 established the judiciary's power to review legislative and executive acts, our courts have a duty to interpret such acts, including congressional legislation. Judicial interpretation is not judicial activism. Judicial activism refers to the practice of judges making rulings based on their own policy views rather than their honest interpretation of our legislators' intent. Here I and the court have abundantly cited the legislature's intent in passing 1437 and the court's duty to interpret and enforce that intent. I'm sure Mr. Farrat did not intend to imply otherwise by his last remarks."

Not addressing the prosecutor's aggressive argument of judicial activism or Hawke's rebuke, the judge went to the next issue.

"Mr. Farrat, how do you address the fact that vital evidence in the state's possession is now missing and Mr. Hawke cannot defend his client because of it?"

"Your Honor, the defendant pled to carjacking. When the judge questioned him on whether sufficient evidence existed to support Guerra's plea to the auto theft, the defendant had plenty of time to state how he wasn't responsible for De Jesus' death. Guerra and his attorney made no such statements.

Instead, Guerra accepted the plea deal. Therefore, the people have a murder committed during a violent felony and the defendant admitted he participated in the armed carjack. What more does this court want?" the feisty prosecutor added.

"Your Honor, may I?"

"Yes, Mr. Hawke."

"The normal sentence in California was three to five years for armed car theft. The judge gave Mr. Guerra, a nineteen-year-old, first-time offender, the maximum sentence allowed for carjacking—nine years. I submit the court did take into consideration the death of De Jesus and he shouldn't now be prosecuted under any co-conspirator standard."

"I agree, Mr. Hawke."

"Further, Your Honor, to proceed after so many years with vital witnesses dead and evidence missing means Mr. Guerra can't get a fair trial under such circumstances. Nor can I provide an adequate defense, which I believe I could if I had all the evidence."

"Nonsense, Your Honor," the excited prosecutor protested. "The defendant can take the stand himself and say exactly what Mr. Hawke coaches him to say."

"Jack, enough. No need to make this personal," admonished the judge.

"Your Honor, Mr. Farrat is playing to the press and through it to potential jurors. The law requires the prosecution to prove its case, not for the defendant to prove his innocence."

"Enough posturing, you two. Mr. Hawke, I get everything you say. And my tentative ruling was to dismiss. However, I am afraid this court will not be able to resolve this very important issue. Gentlemen, I have asked you to put your arguments on the record so the United States Assistant Attorney seated here in court could hear them. I did so because the federal government took over jurisdiction of this case yesterday afternoon. I no longer have jurisdiction. Mr. Guerra is being transferred to the Federal Metropolitan Correctional Center later this morning."

"What?" exclaimed Hawke in a loud voice as he rose. "This is ridiculous."

"I concur," snapped Farrat as he jumped to his feet. "This is most unusual, Your Honor."

"Indeed, gentlemen. I put all this on the record so the public knows what is happening to such an important case. Mr. Hawke's challenge to such a late prosecution and the ambiguity it raises about 1437 are issues the citizenry of this state should know about and demand some sort of an explanation."

"Judge Brown, I must protest," Drew said. "Frankly, sir, I just don't know what else to say."

"Mr. Hawke, this is not the forum . . ."

"I must protest too. The murder occurred in San Diego and state laws should apply," voiced Farrat.

Detective Clayton standing by his side couldn't hold back. "This is a violation of state's rights."

"Gentlemen, make your arguments in federal court, not here. And you, Detective Clayton, are out of order. You will make your feelings known through Mr. Farrat. Do I make myself clear?"

"My apologies, Your Honor. It just slipped out."

"Please have a seat, gentlemen. The Guerra matter is suspended pending the outcome of proceedings in federal court. Ladies and gentlemen, we will now take a ten-minute break," Judge Brown added as he rose to exit the courtroom.

"Hawke, what just happened?" Jack Zane, crimes reporter for the *San Diego Herald*, shouted from his front-row seat behind the defense table.

"I have no comment at this time," came the response. "Please contact my office for an interview at a later time."

A TV reporter began questioning Farrat.

Drew turned and looked at Tre Stout and asked, "Can we exit by the back door? I don't want to face the media right now."

"Ladies and gentlemen, please exit the courtroom. We are in recess. That includes the media," Deputy Stout announced in a loud voice, ignoring Drew as he walked toward the audience, trying to shepherd them all out of the courtroom.

When the assistant U.S. attorney started to leave, Drew walked toward her. "Ms. Jala, how can you take jurisdiction in this case?"

"Mr. Guerra committed a federal crime when he helped steal the BMW."

"What in the hell federal crime was committed that gives you jurisdiction over my client?"

"The carjacked BMW 330i was manufactured in Mexico and shipped for sale into the United States. Under 18 USC 2119, any vehicle 'transported, shipped or received in foreign commerce by the vehicle's owner' and thereafter carjacked is a federal crime."

"How in the world do you know the car was manufactured in Mexico?"

"It's VIN plate begins with '3BMW' and there is a 'J' in the seventh position of the VIN," she replied. "The car was manufactured at the Group Plant San Luis Potosi in Mexico. Once you review our discovery, Mr. Hawke, you will see the victim special-ordered that vehicle only to have it stolen at gunpoint six days after arriving in San Diego. Oh, yes, I shouldn't forget, as the thieves drove away, one of the three leaned out the front passenger side window and fired in the direction of the victim."

Out of apparent frustration, Drew reacted. "Oh, for cryin' out loud, this is ridiculous. Stealing a case of burritos at gunpoint from a Mexican delivery truck could qualify as a federal crime under such reasoning. California should have sole jurisdiction."

Surprisingly, Jack Farrat, who had been carefully listening from afar, joined in, "Hell, yes."

"The judge is correct," Liberty Jala said. "Make your arguments, gentlemen, to the federal magistrate not to me. Good day."

Her quick exit left Farrat and Drew speechless.

Liz sat mute as the three drove back to the Gaslamp Quarter. When Matt turned into the Ace parking lot, Liz tapped Drew on the shoulder.

"This was planned ahead, wasn't it? And you knew about it didn't you?" Obviously upset, she didn't wait for a response. "Why didn't you tell me?"

Any effort to answer was interrupted by Mario Rodriquez, the parking lot attendant.

"Morning, Jefe. Want me to detail this beauty for you?"

"That's okay, Mario."

"In that case, I'll just give it a quick wash. Gotta make sure my abogado has good-looking wheels."

Drew smiled. "Thank you, Mario."

"Drew don't you ignore me," Liz said. "This morning was all part of the plan, wasn't it?"

Drew turned around. "Okay, yes. I think I was very believable, don't you?"

"You're a lousy actor, Andrew Hawke. Even Judge Brown sensed it. He knew what was going on. He wanted Jala to know how he felt."

Drew said nothing.

"Answer my question. I'm right, aren't I."

"You mean about my not telling you?"

"That's exactly right. I worked very hard on all our motions and was all nerves about arguing the bail motion."

"I was told not to by Mancini."

"Since when do you do what anybody tells you . . . you . . . oh, I don't know what to call you. You deceiver."

Drew laughed. "See? I was a good actor."

"That's it. Let me out."

Drew opened the passenger door and stood. As Liz pulled herself up toward the door, Drew offered her his hand. She slapped it away and stormed off toward the office.

"Drew, I think you messed up bad," offered Matt.

"Matt, everything had to be kept secret. Otherwise, we risked Carlos being killed while in the County Jail."

"After Liz cools off you better do more than just explain things. I think you're in the doghouse for sure."

"Young man, since when are you the expert on women?"

"You'd be surprised, boss. Besides, I know enough not to piss off my girlfriend."

The two laughed as they headed to the George J. Keating Building. Once they opened the office door, there stood Liz next to Debbie, who had a stern look on her face.

*Oh, boy, she told Debbie.*

"Before you start in, Debbie, I had to keep the whole thing secret. Mancini said if we didn't, Guerra's life might be in danger. Kiefer specifically told me the FBI believes there are Enforcers in the Sheriff's Department who might try getting to Carlos."

"Nope, not good enough, Andrew. You either trust Liz and me or you don't."

"It isn't that I don't trust you. Once the techs left, our office was subject to outside surveillance."

"Humph. Next time, Andrew Jackson, you think the place is wired, write it out on a piece of paper."

"That's right," said Liz. "Don't let Mancini play us for fools. He wants us divided, not a team. Just because they don't trust anyone doesn't mean we can't trust one another."

"You're right, guys. My apologies."

"So tell us, what's next?" asked Liz.

"Yes, what's next?" added Debbie with a skeptical look.

"I really don't know. Pat wouldn't let me in on it. I think he's trying to protect us. He and Mancini said the less we know, the less danger we're in."

Drew started to walk into his office when Liz stopped him.

"Drew," she called out, "that U.S. attorney said one of the thieves fired a gun at the victim. How can you allow this case to go to federal court knowing someone shot at the victim? The Feds don't give the same amount of credit for good behavior. Carlos could get a sentence far longer than in state court."

"Elizabeth . . ." Drew paused so as not to show his frustration about his actions being challenged again. "Carlos told me that at Manny De Jesus's sentencing, the judge asked him who fired the shot. Manny said he was the gunman. Manny told the court Carlos didn't know he had a gun before he pulled it out and aimed it at the car owner. When questioned further, Manny admitted he had planned to use the gun so they could go joy riding."

"You know that won't fly with the Feds. They do what they want. They won't believe Carlos. Besides, you had the case won in state court."

"I went along with the plan in order to keep Carlos from

being killed in jail." The additional information seemed to calm his associate attorney. "Liz, todays theatrics were all planned by Mancini and Pat. I was just a player. But I had the same concerns as you, so I had Mancini sign a statement saying Carlos was not the shooter. I hope this answers all your questions," Drew said forcibly as he turned again to walk into his office.

"Drew—" Debbie called out. The lawyer whirled about and looked upset by the constant questioning. "Shouldn't you and Elizabeth see Carlos and explain the fast-moving events of the past two days?"

The tension in the lawyer's body eased. "Yes, Debbie, as usual you are right. Liz, are you available now?"

Liz turned and looked at Debbie, who winked and slowly nodded so as not to be obvious.

"Yes, of course. Thank you, Drew."

"Then let's go."

# CHAPTER FIFTEEN

**Wednesday night**

The black Beamer pulled into Marina Cortez at 1889 Harbor Island Drive. Drew got lucky. He found a parking space right next to IVT Yacht Sales. The Artful Dodger was a short walk away on D dock. At his 34-foot sailboat, he changed out of his suit and into surf shorts and an old T-shirt, his favorite workout shirt—a fraying, sleeveless thing with deep-cut side openings that exposed his large biceps, V-shaped lats and taut eight-pack. Drew checked his Apple watch. It was only 6:30; he could still get a bite to eat at the marina deli.

"Evening, Mr. Hawke. Hungry?" asked Annie, the elderly Asian woman behind the counter.

"Sure am. I'm starved. How about a large peperoni pizza. No, wait." Drew paused as he studied the menu board. "Make that peperoni, Italian sausage, bell peppers, and tomatoes. Yup, that's the one."

"One large 'Shipwreck' coming up."

"Annie, I love the names you give your pizzas. They really connote confidence in us captains."

She laughed while Drew watched her pile on the goodies.

"You know, Annie, how about a few mushrooms. I'll pay extra."

"No extra, Mr. Hawke. Some more no problem."

"That's perfect. Thank you."

Drew went over to the refrigerator, opened the glass door, and perused the selection of local craft beers. "Hey, Annie. Is this Olde Ale any good? The ones on the bottom shelf. They're new?"

"It should be. The distributor said it won gold at the World Beer Cup."

"Sold, that's good enough for me," replied Drew as he bent over to pick up the six-pack.

At that moment a familiar voice came from behind. "Nice underwear."

Drew immediately stood, pulled up his surf shorts and turned around to see Mia Lombardi, the woman Drew had been trying for months to build up the courage to ask out. *What beautiful skin. Slightly tanned and not a bit of lousy makeup. Perfect.*

"You got the hungries too?" he asked.

"It's that time of the evening. What's Annie cooking that smells so good?"

"Pizza. Want to join me?"

"What type?"

"Oh, choosey, huh. It's a large Shipwreck."

"Hmm. A bit meaty but okay. The peppers and tomatoes sound really good."

"How about a beer? Ever heard of Olde Ale? It's new," Drew said as he held up the colorful six-pack container of glass bottles. "Annie said it won gold in a competition."

"Now you're making that pizza sound really good," she replied.

"Eat here or at the boat?"

"Which one?"

"How about mine," suggested Drew. "You haven't seen it before."

"Drew Hawke, you are incorrigible," she said with a twinkle, "Why not? I haven't seen your lair yet."

"Lair." Drew blushed. *Man she is direct and tough. But I guess this counts as a first date.*

Just then the pizza came out of the oven. Annie slipped it into its box.

"What's the damage, Annie?"

"No need to pay now. I put it onto your tab. She grinned. "You two go eat while it is hot."

"Thanks, Annie."

Mia carried the beer as they walked down the steep gangway to the dock. "Old shirt," Mia said as she checked him out.

"This raunchy old thing is my gym shirt."

"Fits you good."

"I hate to say it, it's my favorite." Inside he screamed to himself. *Right on, she noticed my bod? Now don't get carried away. Act like you don't know she's checking you out.*

At the Dodger, Drew stepped onto the swim step and offered his hand. She stepped up, grasping his hand but fell against him.

"Thanks. I was more concerned about the six-pack. I shoulda watched my step."

Once inside the cabin, she paused and looked around.

"I'm surprised; this is really big. Actually quite homey," the woman said as she continued to look about. "You've got a Hawaiian flag," she said as she pointed to the flag hanging from the left side of the front bulkhead. "Have you been there?"

"I lived there."

"Where?"

"Lahaina Town."

"But why the flag?"

"Ah . . . a long story. Let's just say it reminds me of an event."

"I'd like to hear the story."

"Nah."

"Don't hold back. You got me down here. Spill it," she demanded.

"Promise you won't tell?"

"Yes. Sailor's oath."

Drew smiled. *Sure. A drunken sailor's oath. The most trustworthy.* "While in college, I went surfing with some friends in Hawaii before spending the last part of my summer in Thailand. That's how I ended up in Lahaina."

"And?"

"Okay. We surfed North Shore on Oahu and then went to Maui."

"You seem to be avoiding something, Hawke."

"Okay, okay. I was riding on the back of a motorcycle when a Lahaina cop pulled me and my college buddy over. He cited me for carrying a surfboard. He said it could hit somebody. I got pissed and refused to sign the ticket so he arrested me."

Mia laughed. "You're telling me he threw you into that old jail, the one next to the famous banyan tree, for not signing a ticket?"

"Yes."

She belly laughed. "What a story." Then she added, "Hey, wait a minute. There's no flag in that jail."

"How do you know?" Drew asked with a knowing look.

"I just do. Where'd you get the flag?"

"Let's just say there was one on the second floor."

Mia thought for a moment. "You didn't? The courtroom on the second floor?"

Drew said nothing. She asked again but more directly.

"Sorry," Drew replied. "I plead the fifth." Immediately he changed the subject. "Pizza's getting cold. How about that beer?"

"Drew Hawke, a second-story burglary! I didn't think you were the type," she said with a look fixated on the young man. Then surprisingly she asked, "Do you have anything stronger?"

"Ah, sure. Tequila, bourbon, vodka . . . you tell me."

"If I'm going to spend the night with a felon, make it a shot of tequila."

*Holy shit. Did I correctly hear what she just said? Be cool dude. Act like you didn't hear it.*

"Well, in that case, how about El Jimador. It's made from fresh Jimador, the best-tasting agave plant, and then immediately bottled, preserving the plant's fresh taste. I usually drink Jack and Coke, but since you're having tequila, I'll do the same."

Without pausing Mia replied. "Good. Add the Jack and Coke as a chaser."

Drew turned and starred. "That's a lot of alcohol."

"Don't worry, Hawke, I can handle it," she added with a smile.

As he poured the shots, Drew picked up the remote and turned on the television.

"You got to be kidding me," Mia exclaimed while observing the TV on the right bulkhead wall. "You programmed it to show a famous painting. Drew, I would have never assumed you were into the arts."

"One of my clients is the largest art publishing house in the country. They gave me this program. It turns your wall TV into a picture frame for the art of the great masters. Here, watch. I'll change the picture."

"That's a Rembrandt," she yelled, pointing at the screen.

"Yes, his famous Night Watch painting."

"Are there others?" Mia asked.

Drew clicked the remote. Without a pause she pointed and said, "The Birth of Venus, by Botticelli," while stepping closer to the 42-inch screen.

"You know your art," Drew praised. "What's this?"

"Samson's Youth by Leon Bonnat."

"And this."

"That's the Women in God by Gustav Klimt. It's so beautiful. And that's De Vinci's famous ceiling in the Sistine Chapel."

Drew changed to another.

"Ah . . . I don't know that one."

"Bouguereau's Rapture of Psyche," replied Drew. "This is Holbein's Henry VIII. Am I going on too much?"

"No, don't stop."

Drew clicked the remote again. "This is . . ."

"Edvard Munch's The Scream," yelled Mia, thoroughly engrossed in the art show. "It's so vivid Drew. The red-orange sky is brilliant."

"It really is, and the guy freaking out is haunting."

"Does the TV make all the paintings look so good?" she asked.

"The TV is digital ultra-HD. The app's instructions say it recreates paintings as if you were in a museum. Frankly, I got to agree."

Drew turned the program to automatic so it would slowly switch paintings on its own. He opened a sink-cabinet door and pulled out two plates.

"There's forks and knives in the draw nearest me," he said and handed the plates to her. "Let's eat on the table."

Mia slipped into the bench behind the cabin table while Drew placed the pizza box next to the plates.

"How about some music?"

"Sure."

"How about something classical to go with the art show. I've got Massenet's Meditation and Beethoven's Romance?"

"You choose."

"Then it is Beethoven's Romance with violin and orchestra."

"Your Jimador, senorita, with a slice of lime and of course the chaser," Drew offered as he slid in next to her.

"Thank you. To art," Mia offered as she raised the shot glass.

"To art, it makes life worth it."

Mia smiled and threw her head back as she downed the shot. The two started devouring the pizza.

"This is really good, Drew."

"Annie always makes the best."

"So what's with all the video and audio on a boat? Or is it simply your floating man cave?"

Drew laughed. "I take the Dodger out all the time. I've sailed her throughout the Channel Islands, many times to Santa Catalina, even down to Ensenada and Cabo San Lucas."

Not to be evasive, he quickly added, "But, yeah, this is my sanctuary, a home away from the loft. When at sea, however, I don't use the Dolby equipment. Whales don't like the vibrations."

"You have a loft!"

"Yes, in the Gaslamp Quarter."

A broad smile came over her face as Drew handed her another slice of pizza.

"Thank you," she replied, looking at the very interesting, if not complicated, man seated next to her. "I don't mean to be rude, Drew, but you are not the normal twenty-something bachelor."

"What do you mean?"

"You're well educated, employed, dedicated to causes—like helping people wrongfully charged—and yet very much interested in the finer things, the arts for instance."

Somewhat embarrassed and wanting to change the subject, Drew asked, "What about you, do you like music?"

"Of course."

"Have you been to the Belly Up yet?"

"Isn't that in North County? Has live shows?"

"Yeah, in Solana Beach. Do you like guitar music?"

"Not sure what you mean. Like classical Spanish guitar, say similar to Paco de Lucia?" Mia asked.

"You are musically versed. Did you study music in college?"

"A little. But I never finished school. I mean I don't have a degree. I'm a few credits short."

Trying not to ask more questions that might make Mia uncomfortable, Drew moved on. "I love flamenco guitar, but I also like electric guitar music. Do you like heavy guitar, I mean music with a lot of guitar finger work?"

"Probably. I usually let my date choose the type of music."

"Oh." Not expecting such a reply, Drew tried to not show his surprise.

"Remember, Drew, I've been at sea a lot and only get satellite radio, so I may or may not know what you're talking about."

Drew nervously laughed. But seeing an opening he went for it. "The Belly Up has some good guitar musicians coming in a couple of weeks. Ted Benoit, a Delta Blues singer and electric guitarist. A little after that Willie Kahaiali'i. Willie's a Lahaina Town guitar extraordinaire famous for his Hawaiian-style rock music. You might like him being as you've been to Lahaina."

Mia smiled. "It sounds like you are really into music."

"Nah, well, yes, I like live performances. If you're up for it, maybe we could go to one of these live performances?"

"Sounds fun, sure."

"Tomorrow we can look at the Belly Up's coming shows and you can choose one. They even have a classical guitar artist scheduled soon."

Mia leaned against Drew. "I look forward to it."

Drew didn't speak. He just smiled and placed his arm around her. *Yes*, a *date. Finally.*

The two talked for hours about each other's interests in life. Drew had dozens of questions about Mia's extensive sailing experience, where her travels had taken her, and to Drew, most importantly, why such adventures. As each revealed their true selves, Drew saw a woman of inner beauty with a perceptive soul—the ability to see things in their true relationship to one another. This was no ordinary woman.

# CHAPTER SIXTEEN

The soft motion of the boat as the tide came in and then out provided the perfect formula for a sound sleep. Suddenly, the early morning silence was broken by a loud noise accompanied by a strong shaking of the boat. Drew's eyes immediately opened. A second louder sound akin to an explosion had him out of bed and into the main cabin. Thick smoke was swirling just outside the bow and its open top hatch. The dark morning sky had streams of red darting through it. Drew could smell smoke through the open portholes.

"Mia, wake up," he screamed. "We're on fire!"

Drew pulled the fire extinguisher off the side of the steps into the cabin and ran up top. There he saw the entire front of the Dodger on fire. Black smoke wafted about the bow as the morning's gentle wind slowly pushed the smoke in a southerly direction toward the yacht next door. He ran forward and sprayed white fire-retardant foam onto the folded mainsail and then on the bow, all the while screaming 'fire, fire,' and Mia's name over and over. "Get out of the cabin, Mia, we're on fire."

She emerged from the cabin in Drew's old gym shirt.

"Mia, you got a cellphone?"

"Yes."

"Call 911. We're on fire, really bad."

A few seconds later, she emerged, coughing as smoke started to fill the cabin. She had a cellphone in one hand and a second extinguisher in the other. She yelled as loud as she could into her phone. "We're on fire. Fire, yes, fire, D Dock, Marina Cortez. Yes . . . hurry, please."

The woman then used the extinguisher on the starboard side walking straight into the fire where it burned along the bow gunwale and down the side of the boat. She aggressively fought the fire under a cloud of white foam retardant and black smoke.

Suddenly, the rolled genoa exploded in red flames all the way up to the top of the mast.

"Mia, get back. The genoa is gone. Get back," he yelled as the genoa fell in flames onto the bow.

The fiberglass on the bowsprit and around the anchor locker began to melt. Burning fiberglass slowly moved toward Hawke along the side gunnel and down the port side of the boat. The fire fully engulfed the bow. Even the water around the bow was on fire. The heat intensified. Drew could feel it against his flesh. The soles of his feet felt burning hot as he shifted from one leg to the other. He retreated backward and emptied the last of the extinguisher's foam onto the mainsail.

"It's no use, Mia," he yelled. "The Artful Dodger is gone. We can't stop it. Get back to the dock."

With black smoke swirling around her petite body, she still stood her ground, trying to fight the fire.

"Get back, Mia. She's a lost cause," Drew yelled again, motioning for her to move back.

"Yes," she mouthed and stepped back, loosing her balance as she tried to retreat through the swirling black smoke. She fell against the safety line and down to the deck, hard.

"Mia," Drew yelled as he threw his extinguisher overboard

and crawled across the top of the cabin toward her, only to see her body disappear in the cloud of thick smoke. The man, coughing uncontrollably, reached forward, trying to find her. Suddenly, he felt something soft. A body.

"Mia," Drew shouted over the roar of the fire and shouts of his fellow boaters rushing to the fire. "Mia, you all right?" He shook her and then hugged the semi-unconscious woman.

Mia's eyes opened. "Drew, I fell. Sorry."

"That's all right. You hurt?"

"My ankle. It really hurts. I don't think I can walk."

She tried to say more but went into a horrible coughing spell, gasping for air. Drew picked her up and carried her aft, through the dense smoke. At that moment, two guys ran along the dock with fire extinguishers, spraying the starboard side and the fully engulfed main sail. Drew could hear voices yelling his name but concentrated on each step as he carried her into cockpit. Huge flames shot into the air. It really was too late. Smoke bellowed out of the bow's open forward hatch—the fire was inside.

"Here, take her," Drew yelled to another man who jumped onto the aft swim deck to help the two. "Be gentle with her," he yelled as the man stepped back onto the dock. Drew turned and steadied himself against the helm as he watched the fire eating more and more of the Dodger.

Drew yelled to two men with extinguishers, "Save the other boats," but the two continued to spray the Dodger with fire retardant. More people ran to assist with fire extinguishers and a long fire hose. Every effort was being used by Drew's fellow boaters to protect the dock and the other boats.

*She's a goner.*

Tears began to run down his face as he watched, adrenaline numbing the searing heat against his body. Black smoke swirled toward him from the cabin's cockpit door. He stood frozen, enveloped in smoke, both hands holding tight to the helm as if fighting to save his ship trapped in a vicious hurricane plunging down the backside of a five-story wave.

Drew could hear the sound of sirens from fire engines entering Marina Cortez's parking lot. The siren and loud horn blasts of a fire tug drowned out the noise of the fire and those fighting it. A Harbor Fire boat came into view as it sped at flank speed down the channel toward the fire. Drew heard more horn blasts and sirens of other fire boats that followed. Drew, gasping for air, just watched, mesmerized by the huge tragedy unfolding around him, until he heard voices. He turned.

"Get off the boat," came the command. "Hey, that's you. Get off the boat."

Drew saw a fireman standing next to Mia, along with an elderly boater who was helping her stand. The fireman yelled one more time as more firemen started connecting hoses.

"Drew, get over here," pleaded Mia.

"Okay. Okay," Drew replied as he stepped onto the Dodger's swim step.

"The fire's inside now," he yelled to the man who was still giving orders as more firemen rushed down the dock. The man ignored Drew and continued to direct action. A giant spray of water shot up into the sky, at least twenty to thirty feet, and showered down onto the Dodger and Drew. He began to shiver as the cold bay water fell on him.

A second water cannon engaged. Soon another approaching fire tug cut loose as both tugs bracketed either side of the burning hulk. Still shivering, Drew leaned forward and tried to look into the cabin. The heat beat him back as black smoke curled out of the cabin's doorway, along with streaks of gray smoke as water fell into the forward cabin through the bow's open hatch and the Dodger's open portholes.

"Sir, step aside." yelled a young fireman, his voice barely audible through his face shield as he and his buddy pushed past Drew and onto the aft cockpit with a huge fire hose.

"Grab my back," the man yelled to his buddy as he turned the hose open, sending a huge volume of water through the door into the main cabin. The two slowly moved forward and down the steps, disappearing into the cabin.

"Hey, you. Are you the owner?" asked the man in charge.

"Yes, sir."

"I'm Captain Svoboda, Harbor Fire. Let us do our job. It's time, captain, to leave your boat."

"Yes, sir," Drew replied as he stepped onto the dock.

"Thank you for coming so quick."

The fire captain did not reply as he ordered where to hook up more hoses to the dock's water hydrants. The huge amount of water showering onto and into the boat turned the black smoke to gray, along with whiffs of white smoke.

Drew felt a hand grab his. "Drew, you're really hot," said Mia, coughing. Just then the elderly woman in the yacht next to the dock's gangway walked up and handed a large beach towel to Drew. That's when he realized he had been fighting the fire naked.

He blushed. "Oh, excuse me. Sorry, ma'am. Thank you."

"Drew, your chest and face are all red," Mia said between gasps for air.

"Did you get burned?" asked the elderly woman.

"A little, I suppose." Drew turned and look at Mia. "Are you all right?"

"I'll live," she haltingly said, going into an uncontrollable cough.

"The Dodger is dying, Mia. Look," Drew hacked out between his coughs, pointing to his boat. "She's sinking at the bow."

A voice to Drew's left said, "It's the water from the tugs' cannons and our hoses. We're basically flooding the inside. She should stay afloat. But you, young man, need to go to the hospital. You're burnt to a crisp and need treatment," commanded Captain Svoboda. He waved to the paramedics, who were running down the dock.

"He's got at least second-degree burns all over his body. He fought the fire naked."

"Yes, sir. What's your name?" asked a paramedic.

"Hawke. Drew Hawke," he answered, coughing. "You should look after my friend. Mia's got a bad cough."

"As do you, Mr. Hawke." The paramedic waved over a gurney and the two medics gently laid Drew down so his burnt skin wouldn't be damaged further. A second gurney followed as more paramedics started examining Mia.

Once at the ambulance, they ordered Drew to lie still while they sprayed some liquid all over his body. It felt unusually cold against his skin. The medics then laid a soft foil-like blanket on him and gently lifted the gurney into the ambulance. Once inside, a medic placed an oxygen mask over his nose.

"Take deep breaths . . . slowly . . . yes, that's it."

Every time he took a deep breath, the wounded man began to cough.

"Are you in pain, sir?" ask he paramedic.

"No drugs. I'll cope," he replied as best he could through the mask.

As the ambulance exited the marina, Drew asked, "Am I burned badly?"

"At least first- and second-degree burns. That spray cools and numbs the burn as well as slightly moisturizing the skin. We use it only on slightly burned people like you. Once at the hospital, the burn unit will take over."

"So I'm going to live?"

"I've seen worse. We're just being cautious."

The sound of the wailing siren and the constant rattle of the equipment in the ambulance bay surrounded Drew as his mind wandered aimlessly. Then a quiet darkness.

# CHAPTER SEVENTEEN

**Several days later**

Slowly, a faint light came and went. As the light grew brighter, noises were heard. Then they were gone. A dark peace always followed, only to be disturbed later as the light returned and faded once again. At times voices sounded in the distance. They seemed familiar. The mind struggled to answer but it couldn't. It was as if he was trapped in a dark fog.

*"Oh, honey, it's Lauren. I love you. Please, please . . . be strong. I . . ." Drew moved his head and his eyes seemed to struggle to open. Then nothing but slow, steady breaths.*

"Come on, young man, wake up. Move your eyes. That's it. Drew it's . . ." Again the voice faded.

"Drew, it's Pat. Come on, son, the doctor says it's time to wake up."

Suddenly, the eyes opened with a blank stare. Then in a soft voice: "Pat. . . there was a fire. I tried my best."

"Sure you did. You're all right now. The doctors say you'll be fine."

"Ah, ha . . . good. I'm tired."

"Sure you are, but it's best you wake up and go home with us."

"Good, I like home."

More voices could be heard. Then, "Mr. Hawke, this is Doctor Nguyen. Look at me. It's time to wake up."

"Oh-kay," came a hesitant reply and his eyes opened. "I'm thirsty."

"Sure you are."

"I've been asleep?"

"Yes, you have."

He licked his lips. "Sorry. How long?"

"No matter. Your body needed the rest."

"I am still tired."

"Good. But Drew it's time to stay awake. You have loved ones wanting to talk to you."

"Drew, honey, it's Lauren. Look at me. You're going to be all right."

"Drew, you just needed rest," a familiar male voice added.

Then his eyes closed. Voices could be heard. They seemed to say, "It is wearing off . . . just another . . ." Then darkness.

Later, another familiar voice. "Drew, Judge Brown postponed the Dave Crumley matter for a month. He said he would make his ruling then, but I have to file a supplemental brief in two weeks. We need to talk about some of the judge's questions.

"Okay. Let's do that tomorrow."

"Good."

There came yet another familiar voice. Drew responded immediately. "Debbie, is that you?"

"Yes, honey. Drew, you scared us. Thank God you are better."

"Is the office all right, Debbie?"

"Yes, the office is fine. Elizabeth has been making appearances, and I am managing the office. Matt says hi. He's in every day, helping. We were all worried to death about you."

"Drew, it's Pat. We know how you love the Dodger. Don't worry. I'm taking care of everything. I'm afraid she's a total loss." Drew's eyes slowly closed as Pat added, "Okay, boy, we'll talk more later."

"Thanks, Pat," he mumbled.

Four hours later, the medication had worn off and Drew was fully awake.

"I'm hungry," he told the nurse. "You got a beer?"

"I'll get you some Jell-O. Dinner is in an hour and a half."

"I want to see Pat."

"Your friends will be here after dinner. The doctor said it was okay."

"Good. But the beer?"

"I'll ask the doctor. But I know she'll say no. Alcohol dehydrates."

"Bummer." His eyes closed once again, but then opened when the nurse returned with three small green Jell-O cups.

"Time for a snack, Drew. I'm going to raise the head of the bed slowly. Just high enough for you to swallow. Here we go. Tell me if it hurts." The head of the bed rose about a foot. "Feel any pain?"

"Nope."

"Now let me feed you the Jell-O."

Drew opened his mouth. An hour later he had a broad smile when he saw the dinner tray arrive. Then when the food dome on his plate was removed . . .

"Is this dinner," he stated.

"Anything wrong?"

"It's so small. And . . . it doesn't look like it will taste good."

"Let's try," she said as she scooped up a spoonful of pureed vegetables and meat smothered in gravy. "Open wide!"

Drew ate the entire meal and asked for more.

"Sorry, Drew. The doctor said this is all for tonight. But I do have some more Jell-O. How about raspberry?"

"Sure. When will I see the doctor?"

"Tomorrow morning."

"Good. Tell him I want to go home."

"I think you are going to stay here a few more days. Your burns have to heal some before you leave."

"Oh, yeah. The fire. How bad did I get burned?'

"Doctor thinks you will be fine. You just have to rest. I'll tell doc you want to go home."

"You're nice." *And a very good looking woman*, he thought. "What's your name?"

"Charlotte. Charlotte Barnhard."

"Sounds southern, Charlotte does, but you don't have much of an accent."

"My, my you are an observant one. I grew up in Atlanta. Moved here when I was thirteen. It's been a while. I've lost my accent, h-o-n-e-y child," she added with a smile. Drew laughed and then added, "Oh, it hurts."

"What does?"

"My whole body."

"The pain killer is wearing off. The burns are talking to you. This is why you should rest. Buzz me if you need more morphine," the nurse said as she placed the call button next to his hand.

"Morphine! I don't think so. I'll live without it."

As Charlotte moved toward the door, Drew raised the covers to look at himself.

"Holy shit. My dick," he exclaimed.

He started to touch himself but the nurse cautioned. "Don't touch your skin. Let it heal. Right now the ointments I applied to your burns help heal the skin and mask the pain. It's best you move as little as possible."

"You applied?"

"Yes."

"Okay, okay. Man it glows down there."

Charlotte smiled. As she turned to walk out, she said, "I mean it. No touching the pee-pee. You don't want it to fall off, do you?"

Drew's eyes widened in surprise and he looked again.

"No, ma'am," he answered.

She laughed, but added as she left, "The more you lift the covers, the more you disturb the skin."

# CHAPTER EIGHTEEN

## The next morning

The door to Drew's room opened suddenly. In strode a beautiful Asian woman in a white coat, followed by Nurse Barnhard.

"Morning, Mr. Hawke. How are you feeling?" the Asian woman asked.

"Ah, good. It hurt a little when I changed positions during the night."

"Yes, of course. Lying on your back is best. The burn is most severe on the front torso."

"I'm sorry, ma'am, but I don't know your name."

"Dr. Kimberly Nguyen. We talked yesterday morning, but you were still coming out of a chemically induced sleep."

"Oh. Are you my doctor?"

"Yes. So let's see how your burns are doing."

Doctor Nguyen put on a pair of gloves and gently pulled back the sheet. She examined the burns closely, at times with a magnifying glass. She paid close attention to the bottoms of his feet. Drew was surprised when she lifted his penis and closely examined it and his testicles. The young man looked at Nurse Barnhard who showed no reaction.

"Very good so far," the doctor said.

"So I can go home?"

"The nurses tell me you want to go home?"

"Yes. When do I leave?"

"Let's talk about your injury first. You suffered first- to third-degree burns to your face and front torso. There are a few areas that are very seriously burnt. It's your feet we are most concerned about."

"How serious?"

"Your feet will keep you here for a while. But I believe you will recover fully."

"Will I be scarred?"

The doctor smiled. "No, you shouldn't. You burned quickly because you weren't wearing clothing. But the flame's burning heat drove you back, lessening the time you were exposed. There will be skin discolorations and what you think are scars. But new skin will grow in and, hopefully over time, you'll be good as new."

"This sounds very serious, Doctor."

"It can be very serious if an infection sets in. Since you have burns over so much of your body, you'll need burn resuscitation and closely supervised skin treatments."

"What is 'burn resuscitation'?"

"Yes. They did say you have a very inquisitive mind. So let's talk about burns. When you suffer a thermal injury, the body experiences both a local and systemic inflammatory reaction. In simple terms, the body reacts with an immediate intravascular fluid effect in the burned and surrounding non-burned areas."

"Okay. I understand."

"Good. In more specific terms, there is a change in the vascular permeability of the normal capillary barriers. Therefore, we have to closely monitor your fluid intake and output."

"Why?"

"If we don't monitor fluid intake, your vital organs can be deprived of necessary fluids— nutrients—and can fail as the body sends more blood to the affected areas. That's why we regulate the amount of fluid intake and initially start a crystalloid IV drip."

"I'm sorry, you lost me. What are crystalloids?"

"Crystalloid fluids are aqueous mineral salts and other molecules that are isotonic to human plasma. It's a solution we initially administer to decrease plasma protein concentrations as the body rushes fluids to cool and repair the burned area. During your resuscitation, we closely monitor and replenish all physiological fluids as the body heals."

"So you're trying to keep me in a homeostatic balance as the body fights my burns."

"Ah . . . yes, generally speaking. We monitor the entire body, including its vital functions."

"Why?"

"Drew, we've learned a lot in the last few decades. It is well documented that organs can fail, resulting in death, from burns in as little as ten to twenty percent of total body surface area. You've suffered TBSA to much more of your body. Though most are second- and third-degree burns, protocol calls for us to monitor fluid intake as we treat your burns. That's why we will be running both antibiotic and fluid replacement intravenously. These are the reasons you will be hospitalized for a while."

Drew looked at his forearm and then the plastic bags on a stand next to his bed.

"What I want to do is start a more aggressive treatment of the burned area," the doctor continued. "Then, as early as possible, we will try some special short soaking baths."

"Sounds like I'm going to be here for more than a while."

"Not really, but we do need you to be cooperative and not aggravate any of your burned areas."

Drew nodded.

"So, Mr. Hawke, is there any diabetes in your family tree?"

"I really don't know. My mother has died and my father is . . . I don't know anything about him."

"Well, your heart is strong and blood tests show very good A1C levels, even for your age group, and you have excellent blood circulation to your feet. We will continue monitoring your vital functions. In the next two to three days, I will have a better understanding of your fluid levels, blood tests results, and healing progress. Let's be optimistic. If you don't develop an infection, how about home in four to five weeks."

"That long?"

"Actually, Drew, if you cooperate, it could be sooner."

"Doctor, I need to talk to my office staff in order to keep my practice going. With your permission, I'll have Debbie bring in a laptop and arrange for visits from certain important people."

"Let's talk about that in two days. Until then you will be restricted to family visits and only during normal visiting hours."

"The only mother and father I have are Lauren and Pat De Luca. They raised me after my mother died. Debbie, Elizabeth, and Matt are my closest and dearest friends. They are family too. They run my office. There is no one else."

"All right. You work things out with Nurse Barnhard. Charlotte runs this burn unit. So be nice to her. She's in charge of you for now."

"Ma'am, I don't wish to be persistent, but I have people facing life and death situations."

"I'm well aware of your criminal practice, Mr. Hawke. You're always in the news. Work with Charlotte. We'll try to be as accommodating as possible. But your treatment comes first. The worst thing that can happen is an infection. So we have to take as many precautions as possible."

Dr. Nguyen started to leave but Drew called out. "Doctor, how is Mia?"

"Who's Mia?"

"She was with me when the boat burned. Is she okay?"

"We don't have a Mia here. Sorry. Anything else?"

Drew shook his head.

# CHAPTER NINETEEN

**Nine-thirty at night**

A figure was barely discernable, masked by the shadows along the side of the house. A car pulled into the drive and a tall man in his fifties exited the driver's door. As he walked toward the front door a voice rang out.

"Clayton."

The man whirled about with his service weapon drawn.

"Tom Clayton, it's me, Pat De Luca."

"Step out into the light," came the command.

"My hands are raised," Pat responded as he emerged into the evening's faint moonlight.

"What the hell! What are you doing here and lurking in the shadows?"

"Put the gun down, Detective. I'm here to talk."

"About what?"

"The De Jesus brothers."

As De Luca approached, Clayton gave another order. "That's far enough and keep your hands visible."

"What do you have to fear from me? I've backed your ass in many a tight spot, even risked my life protecting you. Tom, put the gun down so we can talk freely."

"I'll decide if we talk at all. Say your peace and quickly."

"It's about the brotherhood, the Enforcers."

"Who?"

"The Enforcers."

"I don't know what you're talking about."

"Cut the crap, Tom. We both know who they are, so let's stop the charades. Man to man. No games."

"Say what you came here for. I'm not happy to see you, much less talk to you."

"I'm not wearing a wire. Here, look."

"Uh-uh. Keep your hands out to your side so I can see them. We both know nobody wears a wire any more. This talk is over."

"No, it ain't. I've kept the code for twenty years. Why do you now come after me, even the boy? Because of Guerra?"

"I have no idea what you're talking about."

"Bullshit. You nearly killed the kid trying to send a message. A message which was totally unneeded. I'm not going to say a thing."

"If that's the case, call Hawke off."

"Okay, I'll talk to him. He's burned badly. So give me time."

"I've got nothing to do with what you're implying Pat. This conversation is over. Get off my property. And don't come back."

"Message received. Thanks for the talk, even if it was on your terms."

Pat purposely turned his back to Clayton and walked slowly toward the sidewalk with his hands held out from his sides. He turned left and went down the street, disappearing around the corner.

ooooo

At 7:30 the next morning, Nurse Charlotte Barnhard drizzled

a moisturizing antibiotic ointment all over Drew's burned body as a college-age trainee observed. The trainee smiled at Drew as Barnhard explained the process to her.

*You do get a kick out of embarrassing me*, Drew thought as Nurse Barnhard gently lifted his penis while constantly explaining to the trainee how third-degree burns have to be handled.

*I don't have a bit of modesty left*, Drew concluded as an embarrassed look came over his face.

Noticing Drew's expression, Barnhard continued. "This antibiotic fluid also numbs the skin while moisturizing the burns. It works best on this type of burn, which heals the fastest unbandaged." Her explanation seemed more for Drew than the observing student, as Barnhard commenced to cautiously smear the lotion onto the burns.

At that moment, Drew noticed Pat De Luca standing at the door with a huge smile on his face.

"Oh, no you don't," Drew said. "Charlotte, tell him to wait outside."

"Okay, kid. Call when you're ready," Pat said as he turned away.

The nurse finished by delicately wrapping the severely burned feet in a loose gauze, explaining to the trainee why a serious third-degree and fourth-degree burn had to be covered. Then, with the help of the trainee, they gently pulled the sheet over Drew.

"Mr. De Luca, you can come in," Charlotte called out.

When Pat entered, she admonished him. "Mr. De Luca, you have fifteen minutes only." Turning to Drew, she added, "I don't want you moving around. Let the cream do its job."

"How are the burns coming?" Pat asked as he walked up to the nurse.

"Actually, quite well," she replied. "If things continue improving, he may get his wish to get out of here."

The two woman left, with Nurse Barnhard closing the door.

"Well, Romeo, I see you're getting a lot of loving care."

"Pat," Drew protested, "don't start."

"You do admit those burns could be a lot worse and the treatment far more bothersome than what you're getting."

Without responding Drew asked, "Are you staying safe?"

"Yes. I've taken care of things."

"What do you mean?"

"I talked to Clayton."

"Are you shitting me? How could you risk that? Now they know . . ."

Pat immediately interrupted Drew. "It was part of the plan. Agent Kiefer Mancini was nearby monitoring our conversation. It worked out well. Kiefer said although Clayton didn't make a strong incriminating statement, it was enough to justify the warrant and allow a more intrusive surveillance of the asshole and his communications."

"They had a warrant to tape your conversation?"

"Yes. And Clayton basically admitted they fire-bombed the Dodger to send me a message and for you to get out of the Guerra case."

"Those shitheads. Pat, I'm going to kill the bastards."

"Easy, tiger."

At that moment, there came a knock at the door.

"Not now," Drew yelled.

Not heeding the command, Kiefer Mancini opened the door. Drew started to say something, but Mancini spoke first.

"Just so you know, I arranged for this room. It's totally secure. We've been with you ever since the fire. You're totally safe."

"Like you protected me and Mia at the marina?"

"We were at the marina. We just didn't expect them to come at you by water. I apologize."

"Okay, okay, I get it. I didn't think they knew about the Dodger. What about Mia? Is she injured?"

"We have her under twenty-four-hour surveillance. We had her talk to a counselor. But she's got some burns and lung problems. She's being treated by a pulmonary specialist. She'll be back at her boat soon. She asks about you."

"Man, she must think I'm crap for getting her into such a mess."

"Actually . . ." The agent paused. "I don't know how long you two have been together, but she seems more worried about you than what happened."

A smile crept across Drew's face at the news.

"Drew," Mancini said in a quiet voice, "she plans to move home so her family can help treat her lung problems."

"You seem to be saying the lungs are really damaged."

"I don't know the full extent, but she faces a long period of recovery." Tears welled up in Drew's eyes as he realized the impact the fire had on Mia.

"As far as your burns go," Kiefer added, "our own doctors examined you when you got here, and they consult with Dr. Nguyen daily. I think we can move you out of here soon. The public will be told you are going to another hospital with a special burn unit for rehab. Instead, we'll move you to the burn unit at Camp Pendleton. Once there, the Marine doctors and nurses will manage your care."

"I need to talk to Mia."

"Once at Pendleton, you can communicate with her."

"Is my staff safe?"

"Yes. You can also talk to your staff as much as you need."

"How can that be? Can't the Enforcers see them going onto the base? Those guys will put two and two together. I thought you said once those bastards figure out the FBI is involved our lives would be at stake."

"Drew, we know what we are doing. At the Camp Pendleton hospital, you'll have your own computer and a large monitor for safe remote conferencing."

"Sorry, I'm still upset about losing the Dodger." Mancini started to say more but Drew changed the subject. "Everyone still has their own bodyguards, right?"

"Yes."

"Even Matt?"

"Of course. We gave him two new agents who are now his roommates for the fall semester. So don't worry."

Drew seemed to have an expression of pain as he shifted his weight on the special air mattress.

"If I've answered all your questions, can I tell you what the plan is?"

"Absolutely. Thanks, Kiefer, for including me."

"We think Pat confronting Clayton was convincing enough that they will back off from taking any further actions. With Mr. Guerra in our custody, he will soon enter a plea where he confesses to a trumped up charge and is sent to prison."

"No. You said he wouldn't be charged with anything. The guy is innocent."

"'This whole thing is fake. Solely for public consumption—all the way down to federal prison records showing his confinement in South Carolina. Mr. Guerra and his family are being moved to a new location within WITSEC, our witness protection program."

"What about his kids? Some have college aspirations."

"Mr. Guerra will learn a new trade. We've already discussed this with him and he's agreed. The children are all going to new schools. Miguel will be going to college. He is very excited."

"They can't afford all this."

"The witness protection program covers everything. It's going to be great for them."

"Thank you, Kiefer."

"Now, here's what we do next . . ."

"Not yet."

"What do you mean?"

"Before anything else happens, I want to be healthy enough to participate. You owe me that much. Kiefer, I want to be able to walk and see what's happening."

"Drew, it's best—" De Luca offered only to be cut off.

"No, I know what you're going to say. No. I'm in this, burns and all."

The investigator turned to Kiefer. The two exchanged looks.

"I will check with my superiors," Kiefer responded.

"Kiefer, don't stall me. I want to be in on everything. Otherwise, I'm out of here and screw your ruse of transferring me anywhere. I'm going home."

"Drew . . ."

"Pat, stay out of this. No one can keep me here, much less force me to go along with any Fed plan. I will cooperate only if I can walk and be in on everything. That's it. I don't want to hear anything else."

With that Drew threw back the sheet and pushed himself into a seated position. He repeatedly pushed the remote's call button. Pat looked to Kiefer for help. When a voice answered, Drew demanded, "Bring me my clothes. I'm out of here."

The nurse replied, saying she couldn't do that.

"I don't care what the doctor said, I'm leaving," he protested as his face reddened and veins stood out on both sides of his neck.

"Sure, Drew, sure," Kiefer relented. "I'll do it your way. Please calm down. Besides, the next move is Clayton's, so we should have time."

"How so?" the young man asked, grimacing in pain but still agitated.

"Logic says they will get back to Pat to confirm you are getting out of Guerra's case as Pat promised. I've already arranged a federal public defender to take over representation. Sound good to you?"

"So you'll do nothing until I can walk?"

At that moment a male orderly and two nurses rushed in to the room. One was Nurse Barnhard with a big hypodermic needle.

"It's all right," Kiefer stated. "He's calmed down."

"Yeah. I'm fine. Sorry I lost my temper," Drew added.

Charlotte continued to approach Drew. "What's going on?"

"We've resolved everything," Pat injected. "The boy is good."

"Is that right, Drew?"

"Yes, ma'am. We're good."

Charlotte looked at her patient. Drew was red and sweat ran down his face and chest.

"Gentlemen, it's time for you to leave," she ordered as she handed the hypodermic needle to the male nurse.

"No, Charlotte. Please," Drew appealed. "I'm okay. We've got a few more things to talk about. I swear I'll behave."

The nurse looked at the FBI agent, who nodded in agreement. "All right, but just a few minutes more. And you, Mr. Hawke, must not move," Nurse Barnhard added as she gently assisted Drew onto his back and pulled the special sheet over Drew's body.

Once the medical staff had left the room, Kiefer continued. "Look, I've got to figure out how to announce your condition has worsened. That should make Clayton and the other cops wonder how you can continue representing Guerra. If they don't take the bait and don't contact Pat, then Pat will contact them and say he's convinced you to withdraw for health reasons. Yes, that will work. I like it," the agent added.

"That's a promise, right, Kiefer?"

"Yes. I fully understand your concern. I promise. We'll make an announcement of you withdrawing and the Federal defenders taking over, and then Guerra's plea." Drew held his gaze on the agent and then added, "I want to hear from Wyland. I know he's running the show. Yeah, I want to talk to him in person."

"I will talk to Wyland."

"Good."

"In fact, I'll go right now and tell him what we're doing. In the meantime, keep calm. We can't wait forever."

Kiefer's demeanor appeared grim as he walked out, pulling the door hard after him. Drew slowly tried to shift his body in an effort to ease the pain.

"You all right, Drew?" Pat asked.

"I just hurt all over. I'll be better in a few minutes."

"I'd say you certainly know how to piss people off. I hope you know what you're doing. A lot is at stake for a lot of people."

"So do I. But I just can't lie here doing nothing."

"Okay, I'll back you. We've always confronted things together. This will be no different."

# CHAPTER TWENTY

**Two weeks later**

At 2:30 a.m., a military ambulance approached the back entrance to Kaiser Hospital's emergency department. Two EMTs exited the vehicle and entered the building. Over the next thirty minutes, two more ambulances arrived. During that time two unmarked SUVs appeared and parked at different points along the entrance road to the back of the hospital campus. Two other SUVs had already parked at other points on northbound Interstate 15. An hour later, a camouflaged Humvee pulled up. Three Marine lieutenants exited the vehicle and proceeded through the back door to the ER. A captain and two enlisted Marines stood by the Humvee. All the Marines wore holstered sidearms.

Soon, two EMTs, led by a Marine lieutenant, exited the ER. They pushed a gurney with an apparent patient covered with a sheet. The gurney was lifted into the nearest ambulance, and the three men got into the ambulance. Shortly afterward, two more similarly covered gurneys emerged. Each gurney was escorted by EMTs and a Marine lieutenant. All four vehicles started their engines and proceeded to the hospital's exit. As the column headed toward Interstate 15's northbound on-ramp, the two unmarked SUVs followed at a distance.

Hours later came a voice. "Good morning, Mr. Hawke." It was a man in a white medical coat. "I see you are awake. Welcome to Camp Pendleton Hospital."

Drew stared at the man. "I'm where?"

"Camp Pendleton. I'm Colonel Stewart Stroud. I'll be supervising your treatment."

"Remind me, why am I here?"

A voice from behind the colonel answered. "You've been moved here for advanced burn rehab."

"Who is it?"

"Oly. Just relax and get used to your new surroundings," Wyland replied as the U.S. attorney walked into view. Drew looked surprised.

"You said you wanted to talk to me," Wyland stated in his normal, condescending tone. "Doctor, do you mind? Drew and I need to talk in private."

"Yes, of course, Mr. Wyland."

At that moment a Marine lieutenant dressed in work fatigues stepped through the door and ordered, "Atten-hut." The doctor immediately came to attention as a rod-stiff Marine general strode past the lieutenant.

"As you were, gentlemen. Good morning, Colonel Stroud. I see we have a special patient?"

Yes, sir. The civilian we've been preparing for, Mr. Andrew J. Hawke."

"Young man, I hear you suffered some severe burns."

Upon seeing the general's rank, Drew immediately sat up. "Yes, sir," Hawke replied.

"Mr. Hawke, please lay back," came a request from Doctor Stroud.

"Sorry, sir, for interrupting. But it is very important he not move and remain supine, especially right after hyperbolic treatment."

"You started chamber treatment?"

"Yes, General. He was sedated for the trip and since I have closely monitored his civilian treatment, I felt an initial treatment was advisable while he was still asleep."

The general looked to Drew. "Young man, how did you get burned?"

"I tried to put out a bad fire, sir."

"And how did that fire start?"

"General, that is confidential. Drew you are not to answer," demanded Wyland.

The general immediately turned and looked at the civilian.

"And who might you be?"

"Oliver T. Wyland, United States attorney for the Southern District."

"Well, Mr. U.S. Attorney, this is my military base, and you will speak only when spoken to."

"General, I must object. Hawke is under FBI protection."

"Mr. Wyland . . ." The general paused, obviously angered, but then asked, "That's your name, right?"

"Yes."

"Mr. Wyland, by whose authority do you enter this military facility and interrupt its chain of command?"

"Ah . . . by order of the President of the United States and Secretary of the Navy," replied the U.S. attorney, with a sarcastic smirk.

"I'm well aware of my chain of command, Mr. Wyland. Who may I ask is your immediate boss."

"The United States Attorney General."

"That, Mr. Wyland, I already know. For your information,

I have graciously accommodated his request. Now that that's clear, do not give me orders. This is my base," the general commanded.

Before Wyland could protest further, Drew spoke up. "Sir, I don't know exactly who started the fire, but I had to try to save my boat, sir."

"I see. Your respectful answers seem to indicate you are familiar with military ways," stated the general.

"The man who adopted me, my father, he served in the military, sir."

"Which branch?"

"Army, sir."

"And may I ask his rank?"

"Ah . . . sir, I've asked him several times but he never told me."

"Why would he not state his rank?"

Drew looked a loss for words, then he replied, "He always said in his Delta unit rank didn't matter. No disrespect intended, General."

"Delta Force you say."

"Yes, sir."

"Has your father ever told you about any of his special joint operations?"

"No, sir. But I've overheard members of his unit talk about HALO or MFF jumps, apparently on special missions. As a young teenager, it sounded exciting."

"I bet it did. Do you intend, Mr. Hawke, to serve yourself?"

Drew again seemed not too sure how to answer. Just before the general started to speak, he replied, "I was nominated to attend Annapolis but decided to go to college and then to law school instead."

"And which law school did you go to?"

"I went to Santa Clara University. It's a Jesuit school."

"Oh, I'm well aware of Santa Clara. My daughter goes there. Mr. Hawke, did the fire have something to do with your law practice?"

Wyland once again started to speak but hesitated this time. "I'm afraid so, sir."

"I can see why the government is so interested in you. If I may give you a word of advice, don't let this Wyland guy abuse you."

"Oh, I know how Mr. Wyland manipulates. My guard is up."

"Ha, you are indeed an interesting young man. Too bad the Navy didn't win you to our ranks. I think it's our loss. Well, good luck, Hawke. I'd shake your hand but I think Doctor Stroud would protest out of fear I may contaminate your burns."

The general turned, acknowledged Colonel Stroud, who snaped to attention, and brushed past Wyland without any word to the obviously perturbed U.S. attorney.

Two days later, Drew sat in front of the computer he insisted Wyland give him. But what use was it? It dawned on him the Feds probably bugged it. If he were to email Julian and Mario, it might give away their plans. So, he only used it to communicate with his law office, and even that had to be generic.

In between his daily routine of a burn bath and one of the two HBOT sessions, he read *The Pendleton Scout*, Camp Pendleton's newspaper. The article that had his attention was headlined: "Three Marines injured in a rollover accident." As Drew read on, he began to put together how he was secretly transported to the Marine base. *What a coverup strategy*, he thought. After reading the article, Drew exited Google and opened a file entitled "Diary."

The diary was the idea of the Marine psychiatrist. A way to deal with the trauma of the fire and the loss of his beloved yacht. But the lawyer had another purpose for his first diary. He used it to document everything he could remember about that evening. All in hopes of finding those who nearly killed Mia and himself.

The diary held his summation of every news article about the fire; every statement and question asked of him by the FBI before and after the fire; every statement and question by the Harbor Police and arson investigators; and the unique cover story about Drew's badly burned body and how the burns forced him to withdraw his representation of Guerra. All the way up to Guerra's federal prosecution and imprisonment. He had created a tight time line, from the time he first interviewed Guerra's son to that day's new entry.

"Excuse me, Mr. Hawke," interrupted a male nurse.

"Yes, Jaylen."

"The gentleman you requested is here."

"Send him in."

"Don't forget, sir, you have your first Hyperbolic Oxygen Treatment in forty minutes."

"I understand, Sergeant, but this is a longtime friend, so stall the HBOT as long as possible."

The Marine nurse smiled.

*Damn good man, that Jaylen.*

As a Hispanic man walked in, Drew rose from his chair.

"Mario! Thank God you're here."

"Jefe, you okay? We heard about the fire and feared for you."

"Got a bit crispy but I'm getting better fast. Pressurized oxygen does wonders."

Before Mario could say more, Drew motioned for him to come close.

"Look, Mario, I need you to help me to the bathroom."

Mario looked at his friend.

"I got to pee, Mario," Drew said as he grabbed his friend's arm. Once close, the lawyer whispered in Mario's ear and the two slowly walked to the room's bathroom. Inside, Drew closed the door and turned on the sink faucet.

"I don't know if they are listening," he said in a low voice. "But we gotta talk in secret." Mario seemed confused. "I mean whisper. They are probably listening."

"The Marines?"

"Sheesh. Yes and for sure the FBI."

Mario nodded.

"I hope the Feds don't know what you and Ramirez are doing."

"Not yet," Mario whispered. "But Julian say they are onto him."

"Hmm. Does that mean we need to shut it down?"

"Nah. He say he got them chasing all sorts of fake servers."

"Did Julian's surveillance pick up the fire?"

"Oh, yeah. Jefe, you are el amante romantico."

"Amante romantico? Oh, shit, I never thought you could hear Mia and me."

Mario smiled.

"When I'm out of here we got to fix that. But right now I need to know if you caught the bastards who fire-bombed the Dodger."

"Sí, Jefe. Julian got reconocimiento. But the camera only caught one. The driver, he was in the dark."

"There were two?"

"See, I saw the video. They were in a small dingy."

"What type of dingy?"

Julian, he say it was an Eagle dingy."

"A rigid dingy," clarified Drew.

"Yes, Jefe."

"Did Julian ID who was in it?"

"Very dark, Jefe. The driver, he wore a hoody and mask."

"But Julian did try facial recognition though, right?"

"Sí. Sorry, Jefe, I forget some times to do English. Yes, but he only got the one who threw the fire things. The other's face, the driver, he was hidden."

"Who threw the fire bombs, Mario?"

"A pig. One of the cops that patrols the barrio. A real poli malo. He thumps Hermanos whenever he can. Very vicious hombre."

"Can you write down his name for me?"

"Julian already did. Here."

Drew lingered over the handwritten name. "That bastard. I'll kill him."

"See, Jefe, we're ready to help," Mario answered out loud.

"Sheesh," Drew whispered. "I didn't mean to sheesh so loud. Sorry, Mario."

The two talked a few more minutes. Drew flushed the toilet and turned off the sink. Back in the room, Drew hugged Mario.

"Don't forget, I will call when I'm ready to go home."

Mario smiled. "I will come quickly."

"Mario, the woman that was in the boat with me, how is she?"

I don't know. Word on the street, the smoke hurt the pretty woman bad."

"Nothing more?'

"No, Jefe."

Drew pulled Mario close. "Ask around, please."

Mario nodded.

"You're a good friend. Now go. But watch your backs."

"I'm fine, Jefe. Don't worry."

# CHAPTER TWENTY-ONE

**Weeks later**

Doctor Stroud had his hand around Drew's upper arm as the two slowly walked down the hallway.

"You know you are leaving too early."

"What do you mean, Doc. Look at me."

"Yes, yes, you're doing well, but your feet are not fully healed."

"I'm fine."

"You know, if I say you can't leave, they won't let you go?"

"Come on, Doc, don't do that. We've had this talk for a week now. I promise I will do everything you told me. Soak my feet in the burn solution and rub on that cream."

"And especially the soles and don't forget to elevate them twice an hour."

"Yes, sir."

""And I need to see you in four days."

"Yes, sir. But I thought the FBI didn't want people to know I've been here or where I've been treated."

"That's all settled. I talked to Agent Mancini. He agreed."

"Then, Doc, we're good to go."

"Okay, you've walked far enough. Jaylen, please help Mr. Hawke into his wheelchair." As the male nurse assisted, the colonel added, "Remember, when you get home, no more than twenty minutes on your feet at one time until I see you again. The whole idea is to test them for the first few days. That includes standing. No shoes for the first week, and thereafter only if they don't hurt."

"Doctor, I'm doing much more than that here. Trust me, I know when to rest."

"I understand. I'm very proud of how you've cooperated with your treatment. I just don't want you to fall back as you face day-to-day problems from your practice."

"Sir, you guys have been great. I promise I will use a wheelchair if I have to go to court."

The three rounded a corner into the lobby. There Drew was surprised to see his treatment team and other staff anxious to say goodbye, some holding goodbye and congratulation balloons.

Drew immediately stood and walked over to them. He started shaking hands, thanking each one for their care. He paused to have a humorous conversation with one particularly attentive nurse only to have Nurse Barnhard step out of the line.

"Remember, Drew, what I said about intimate relations. Off limits for at least three more months."

Drew blushed with embarrassment as obviously all heard.

Just then, "Atten-hut," came a command as the base general in full Marine dress blues walked through the hospital's double front doors.

He immediately removed his cover and walked up to Drew. "I see you have decided to leave us."

Drew stood erect and smiled. "Yes, sir."

"Colonel, is he fully healed?"

"No, sir. But he insists on leaving."

Before the general could speak, Drew defended his decision. "Sir, my duty is to my clients and the protection of my loved ones. I think you know what I mean, sir."

"Yes, I do. You are doing something I am quite familiar with. Duty calls."

"Thank you for understanding."

"That Wyland fellow, don't forget my warning. To him, you and your friends are expendable as long as he gets what he wants."

"I know, sir. That's why I need to leave now."

"Ha. You would indeed make a fine Marine. Good luck, young man." The general extended his hand and shook Drew's vigorously. Drew didn't know what to say.

"I see you have impressed members of my hospital staff. I leave you to your goodbyes, Mr. Hawke." The general started to turn but stopped. "Don't forget, Mr. Hawke . . ." The general took one more look at a man he knew he wouldn't see again. "I am here to assist in any way I can. But, frankly, I don't think you will need anyone's help."

In a somber voice, he added, "Remember, don't forget who you are dealing with. Till we meet again."

With those final words, the general did a smart about face and left the way he came in.

When Drew reached the end of the line of well-wishers, Jaylen spoke. "Please be seated, sir. I need to assist you to your vehicle.

Outside, Drew couldn't believe what he saw. "Matt, what are you doing here?'

"I'm your personal chauffer home."

A huge smile spread across Drew's face as he took in his special ride, including the colorful scene of a surfer shredding a huge wave on the side of Matt's van.

"Damn, Matt, I can't wait to hit the surf."

"Drew," forcibly admonished the colonel, "that will not happen for months. The ocean is full of bacteria."

The young man immediately changed the subject. "Doctor, I thought the FBI would take me home."

The colonel smiled at the not-so-subtle effort. "Apparently not. Isn't this better?"

"Oh, yeah. Much better. May I walk to the van?"

"Let's just wheel up and help you into the van. I'd feel a lot better."

That is exactly what they did. Once inside, Drew gently leaned back in the front passenger seat.

"Morning, Drew."

"Oh, no," Drew said, recognizing the all too familiar voice. Drew started to look back.

"Let's keep you looking forward. This way it looks like it's just you and Matt."

"Mancini, where's the rest of your army?"

"They're positioned close. My team will follow from a discreet distance. Sit back and enjoy your new freedom."

"Amend. A-a-m-e-n-d," the young man sung out. Still looking forward, Drew asked, "How is Mia?"

"She's recovering. Don't worry. I know you like her. We will take good care of Mia."

"When can I see her?"

"I don't think she wants to see you, Drew."

Drew immediately turned to look back into the van.

"Drew, look forward," came a stern request.

"Okay, okay. But what do you mean?"

"When she left to go home, she told me not to tell where she is going."

"Bullshit. Mia wouldn't say that."

"I'm just telling you what she asked me to pass on to you."

"Where is she, Kiefer? Don't play stupid. You know where she is."

Kiefer remained silent until Drew turned and faced the agent. "Well?"

"She's in WITSEC."

"The federal witness protection program?"

"Yes."

"Where did you guys put her?"

"I don't know. Once a witness gets into WITSEC, nobody knows except her personal handler. And don't ask. There's no way I can ever find out. The program is closed even to agents like me."

"Would Wyland know? Or even Finnigan?"

"Absolutely not. Not even they nor any other federal employee will ever know."

"As soon as this is over, I'm going to find her."

"I wouldn't advise that, Drew."

"Why?"

"You're a marked man. As is Pat and the others. If you do find her, she's an easy mark to get to."

"You mean they might kill her?"

"Yes. To get even, they might make an example out of her in order to send a message to you and your friends. I told her she must disappear."

"Did she agree?"

"It was the only way to protect her parents. We gave her a new identity. You'll never find her."

"No!" he screamed as the FBI agent's words hit home. The young lawyer hung his head low, "No. God no."

Drew fell silent. The hour ride seemed to take forever as the morning traffic was thick. Once at the loft, Matt punched in the code to the back gate. The van pulled into Drew's parking slot and everyone started to exit.

"Hey, Matt, do you mind if I go up on my own? I'm exhausted. We can talk tomorrow," Drew said in a low, almost inaudible voice. "Let everyone know I want a calendar meeting. I need a case-by-case review, so tell everyone, be prepared."

"Sure, boss."

"Drew we need to talk," Mancini said.

"Kieffer, I'm really tired. How about you come by the office."

"Tomorrow?"

"Yes, and have Pat join us. But right now I'm looking forward to a nice quiet sleep in my own bed."

"I understand. See you tomorrow at eleven."

"Thanks for all your help."

Drew stepped down from the van and walked to the elevator. The old finger scanner still worked. As he rode up to the third floor, the van exited with Matt and Agent Mancini.

The elevator came to a jarring halt. *They still haven't fixed this thing.* Drew pulled back the gate and looked into the eye scanner he installed just before the fire. The biometric system recognized his retina's blood vessel patterns and opened the door.

As he entered he was greeted by a familiar voice. "Morning, Drew."

"Morning, Tami."

"You've been gone 57 days, 11 hours, and 42 minutes. Welcome back."

"Thanks, Tami, glad to be home."

"Should I turn on the Keurig?"

"Yes, that would be good."

"Coffee on. You need to choose a K-cup. Water level good for two cups of coffee."

A smile came over his face as he looked around. *Same old place. Same old Tami. Really nice to be back.*

"Welcome home, son."

Startled, the young attorney swung around in the direction of the loft's kitchen. "Pat," how'd you get in here?"

Not waiting for an answer, Drew rushed to Pat and hugged him tightly.

"Nice to see you're healing so well," Pat said. "Lauren and I have been worried, but they said I shouldn't visit once you went to Pendleton."

"I understand, Pat."

The investigator immediately indicated Drew shouldn't talk loudly. In a low voice, he said, "The loft may not be safe."

Drew indicated he understood.

"Remember, Drew, everything is bugged, or we must assume it is. We've got to look out for ourselves."

"That's more or less what the general said when I was leaving the hospital."

"General?"

"Yes. He looked in on me several times. Nice man."

"I know. He actually called me. He was very impressed with you." Pat quickly added, "I didn't tell him anything."

"One thing's for sure, he doesn't like . . ." Drew leaned really close. "O-l-y." The two laughed as he whispered how the general tore into the U.S. attorney.

"Pat, what's going on? Don't hold anything back. I left early to find out."

Pat looked down.

"Come on, Pat, I have a right to know. I'm in this mess too."

In a very low voice, he said, "They contacted me and want to meet."

"Where?"

"At a cabin in East County."

"When?"

"They said I will be contacted."

Drew stepped very close and in a low but forceful voice, said, "I'll go with you."

"No. It's best only me."

Pat refused to say anything more. He constantly indicated the loft wasn't safe. When Drew persisted, Pat kept changing the subject.

Finally, Drew had had enough. The lawyer stepped back and with a stern, serious look, said, "Pat, if you don't keep me informed, I will never talk to you again. I mean it. This is bullshit."

Pat stiffened and stared at his young man with a shocked look.

"I mean it, Pat. You told me we always faced things together. You made me promise as a kid never to hide anything from you. I promised. That pledge has always been a two-way street."

"Okay, kid. Okay. When I'm contacted . . ." The man stepped forward and whispered, "Mancini and I will come see you. Until then, we shouldn't be seen together."

Drew nodded. He extended his hand to Pat. Instead of shaking the hand, Pat pulled him close for a hug.

As they embraced, Drew's mind raced. *Pat never shook my hand. He doesn't want me involved. Both he and Lauren would die to protect me. He's going it alone!*

Finally, Drew asked about Lauren. After reassuring Drew she was fine, Pat said he should go. They hugged again and the man left. Both men knew what they had to do.

# CHAPTER TWENTY-TWO

## Later that night

Instead of going to bed, Drew sat up wide-eyed, anxiously waiting.

*Where are they. It's 9:12 p.m.,* Drew worried as he fidgeted in his soft leather chair. *Did they talk to Matt? Was I too convincing about needing to sleep?*

Just then Tami announced, "Drew, there are two men at the elevator. They're asking to come up."

Drew rose and walked to the computer screen. "Yes, Tami, let them come." Drew watched the monitor as the two rode up to the loft. "Unlock the door, Tami."

"Door unlocked."

The door opened, and Mario and Julian entered with two large suitcases. Julian Ramirez immediately raised a finger to his lips. Drew nodded. The two set their cases down. Julian took out a handheld device and began to scan the room for covert audio-video surveillance capability, including outside surveillance. Julian then connected a laptop to Drew's computer and began a safety scan. He nodded, turned to Drew, and smiled. Once again, he put his finger to his lips. Fifteen minutes later he said, "Better."

The two then set up another laptop. A few minutes later, he announced, "Now we can talk."

With Julian's innovative cone of silence complete, the three sat down. Drew was the first to speak.

"Julian, I've got all sorts of questions about what you just did, but we really need to talk about Pat and the fire. I need to see the entire film your cameras picked up."

"Mr. Hawke," Julian answered only to have the young lawyer interrupt.

"Please, Julian, we have known each other for several months. You don't have to be so formal."

"Yes, sir. They used an oxidizing accelerant mixed with an igniter and fuel whose flash point was well in excess of 212 degrees. At such high temperatures, the fiberglass on your boat quickly melted. Your extinguisher was woefully inadequate to smother such a fire. You're lucky you weren't burned worse than you were."

"Good explanation, but I'm really interested in who they were."

"Sure, but I think you should know why the fire was so damaging. The arson reports suggests that those who fired your boat knew what fuel to use to do the greatest damage with the least amount of fuel."

"How do you know this?"

"I hacked into the fire department's records on the fire and talked to several friends who know about such things."

"You seem to be saying whoever did this knew what they were doing."

"Exactly. They knew how to burn a fiberglass boat, and quickly. Mario told you who the guy was that threw the devices, but I think you need to worry more about the brains behind the bombing."

"Any ideas?"

"I think you are dealing with more than bad cops. Maybe

someone with experience in chemicals, or even a fireman who specializes in arson investigations."

"Jefe, what Julian told me is we are up against more than a group of bad pigs who terrorize Mexicans."

"I see. That fits with what the FBI told me. Based on the fire, you suggest the corruption extends beyond the police and a few dirty politicians."

"Yes, Mr. Hawke. Corrupt money does buy many people."

Drew was surprised by Julian's mature reasoning. "How does this change our plan to protect Pat and my staff?"

"It doesn't. But we should now look for anyone suspicious. Not just cops. Here's where I think we are at. With the FBI providing physical protection, I believe your staff is safe. More important, we are still able to monitor the FBI's surveillance of your staff and investigator's cars, homes, and phones."

"Help me here. Refresh my memory."

"Remember how I hacked into the FBI's computers and how they use your car's GPS system? That was the open door to avoiding their anti-hacking system. I've embedded code into their computer programs, monitoring their surveillance of you and your friends. I know what they know about Pat and your staff's activities."

"Mario said they were onto you. Is that true?"

"Yes. They are now running all sorts of anti-virus and screening programs because they think something is wrong, but they don't know what."

Julian paused. "You see, Mr. Hawke, they have a Catch-22. Their system perfectly tracks everyone's cars, homes, phones, and activities. Efforts to detect outside hacking or something that compromises their programs has proven unsuccessful. The code is too deeply embedded. Their only choice is to pull their computers and put in all new equipment and surveillance programs to do the same accurate monitoring the current system does. This they won't want to do since they are in active surveillance. The easiest conclusion to come to is that they have an inhouse software error. An error that is giving off false alarms."

"Okay, I understand. But here's the real problem. Pat is purposefully not including me in his efforts to get incriminating evidence on Clayton and Shaughnessy. Plus, the FBI is giving me lip service about me being a part of their plan with Pat. We are in essence on our own."

"That's not much different than what we originally thought. The system I've set up should let us know what the FBI is doing and how they intend to use Mr. De Luca."

"I understand. How much lead time will your system give us when they decide to execute their sting? I've got to be there to protect Pat."

"As I said before, short of you following your friend, there is no way to know. You'd have to literally camp outside his home and be ready to follow at any time."

"Jefe, Julian and I have been talking about this. He says he should be able to tell us when and probably where they intend to act. I've got friends who have agreed to act on a moment's notice to go where Pat intends to meet with those guys. These are good men used to dealing with bad hombres."

"Drew, once we know where they are to meet, I have mobile equipment that allows us to listen and even see inside where they intend to meet," Julian said.

"How good is this equipment?"

"The effectiveness of the equipment depends on where they meet and the type of construction material used at the meeting place. If it's a normal home, then you will know exactly what is going down."

Julian turned to Mario. "Please explain to Drew what your group of friends can do."

"Sí, Julian. Jefe, myself and some friends have been following Pat in shifts, day and night. Julian gave us laptops so we can stay close but out of sight."

"Actually, Drew I programmed those laptops so the FBI's surveillance of Mr. De Luca through their cameras, phone monitoring, everything, are all on the laptops. This allows Mario's group to be close enough to act without the Feds, Pat, or anyone else, seeing them."

"I have a laptop," Drew said, pointing to his work desk.

Anticipating Drew's next question, Julian said, "Sure, I can program it too. And I can set your iPhone for alerts. That way you don't have to leave the laptop open all the time."

"Good. There's an FBI agent now working in my office. I don't want her getting into my laptop."

"It's good that you told me. I'll put in a new security ID that only you can open. And that will prevent access when your laptop is connected to the office's server."

"All right. Guys, good job. But, Mario, I'm worried about you and your friends getting involved."

"No worry, Drew. We can handle ourselves. If we can survive prison, we can handle a few pigs."

Drew shook his head. "Mario, that's exactly what I don't want you to do."

"Jefe, we are exactly the right people to deal with these assholes. Don't worry, we won't get caught."

"Mario, no . . ."

"Drew," persisted Mario, "we got the muscle and all the backup we need."

Julian spoke up. "Mr. Hawke, you yourself said you don't

trust the Feds. It's either them or your friends. Frankly, I'd trust Mario, if I were you."

"I guess I don't have a choice. For now, okay. But all this digital stuff is vulnerable. Any computer program can be hacked. The Feds aren't stupid."

"True. It's my job to keep it functional and accurate. I can do that."

"How will you guys find the time to do all this?"

Mario spoke up. "We already discussed this. This is important, Drew. We are committed."

"I don't know what to say."

"Just say yes, Jefe. That's all we need."

"Okay, it's a go. But you two coming here means the Feds will now run your backgrounds, probably bug your cars, whatever. So we have to disguise why we're in contact. From now on, you are only friends who bring me food, water, anything innocuous. I'll even have you guys drive me to the office and my medical appointments. But, neither you," pointing to Mario, "or any of your friends can follow me. That would give it all away."

Both Mario and Julian nodded. "Jefe, we good."

"And no phone conversations between you, your friends, or me. I've got FBI agents following me everywhere."

"I said we we're in one hundred percent. I already planned on doing what you want. Julian figured we'd have to keep our distance."

Drew, overwhelmed by the loyalty, smiled. "I don't know what to say but thank you."

"Julian pointed to Drew's computer. "Just so you know, the Feds are monitoring your loft computer. That includes its program and the biometrics you use to secure entry to the loft.

And, they can listen to everything that is said in here through your computer."

"Even now?"

"No. I temporarily blocked everything when I came in."

"Damn. Pat was here earlier. We whispered but could they hear us?"

"They sure could. Also, the FBI is planning something next weekend. I don't know what. As the weekend approaches, we may learn more."

"No worry, Jefe. I and my friends are ready to move."

"Drew, as soon as I learn more, I will tell you and Mario immediately."

The three talked for nearly an hour. Each time Drew raised a potential issue, Julian and Mario reassured him they were prepared. Finally, the three looked at each other and smiled. "Drew, we are as prepared as is humanly possible."

"Julian, you are right. Thank you, guys. You are really good friends."

"Before we leave, I've got to install a new app in your computer. The program will take you to the dark web and one of my computers. When you use the app, you can email, text, and talk to Mario and me."

"What happens if they hack in?"

"I'll know if they try. Don't worry, I'll keep everything safe."

"Julian, as soon as you install the app to my computer, they'll know it was you. I'm sure they watched you come in."

"I'll program it to turn on in the morning before you go to work. That way they'll think it was you."

*I thought I was computer savvy. But, man, this Julian guy is some wizard—the devious type.*

Julian installed the new programs and showed Drew how

to operate his computer and laptop, and his iPhone and Apple watch, without alerting anyone to the new apps. Then they said goodbye.

# CHAPTER TWENTY-THREE

**One week later**

The black BMW slowly wound its way through the mountainous, high desert roads of East San Diego County. Julian's program showed the route of Pat's car. Drew followed minutes behind, just as planned. Ahead lay the police chief's ranch, the place where Pat was to meet the Enforcers. The burner phone next to Drew vibrated.

"Yes, Julian?"

"A car just arrived. Three guys went inside. That means there's at least four people now inside the main house."

"Do you know who they are?"

"The one that's been there since late morning seems to be the chief of police. The rest probably cops. But, Drew, the situation is getting very dangerous, too many of them."

"What do you mean?"

"Those two other men who arrived an hour earlier took up positions on either side of the driveway into the ranch. The way they've hidden themselves, their dark clothing and scoped rifles, I think they're snipers. I had to move from my position of surveillance further away so they couldn't see me."

"Where are you?"

"Still across from the ranch entrance, but further up the mountain in a thicket of pines."

"Can you see the main house and out buildings?"

"Yes, I've got a powerful scope. It's a Guide TS large-diameter lens, thermal capable with a refresh rate of 50Hz."

"Julian, I don't know what that means but can . . ."

"It means I clearly see everyone in the house and their movements through the large ceiling-to-floor front windows and their thermal movements through the walls," he responded, somewhat annoyed about being interrupted. "And I can now see the road coming up the mountain from the west, and its sharp downward slope into the desert to my right. It's a much better position."

*Man, too much tech stuff.* "Thank you, Julian. I guess that means you are following what's happening inside?"

"Yes."

"Can you show me where the snipers took up position on my laptop?"

"Stand by."

Drew pulled the Beamer to the side of the road. A second screen popped up next to the GPS route guidance map.

"I see it," Drew said. "Julian, those snipers could shoot Pat as soon as he turns into the driveway."

"Sure can. Should we tell Pat it's a trap and abort the mission?"

"Have the snipers seen any of our men?"

"No. Once they arrived, I put everyone on silent text mode. We're all well hidden from view."

"Snipers, hugh!" stated Drew as he considered his options.

"Mario's men can take them out if you give the order. I moved his rifle teams so they are behind the cop snipers.

They're now camouflaged about thirty yards behind. We have clear shots on both. But there's more."

"Now what?"

"The Feds must be here. Just a few minutes ago I saw two UAVs. One's a tethered, high-altitude quadcopter. They're the type used by the Feds."

"Two?"

"Sorry, Drew. I should have anticipated someone would use aerial surveillance. Those could even be police. There's no way you can come in without them seeing you."

"Have the UAVs seen you?"

"We're really well hidden. But, Drew, if they have thermal sensing cameras, they'll see you and the cop snipers."

"Anything you can do about that?"

"Our sniper team has thermal blankets over them, but not our other men by the house."

"Where's Mario?"

"He's up by the house. Look, Drew, should we tell Pat it's a trap?"

"I don't know, Julian. He doesn't know we're following him. That's why you bugged his car with a tracker. Do you still have access to all federal surveillance?"

"Yes."

"So Mancini's plans for using Pat haven't changed?" Drew asked.

"Doesn't seem so."

"Drew, there's too many guns. Let the Feds handle it."

"Julian, the Feds don't give a shit about Pat as long as they get the Enforcers."

"Sure, but the Feds are supposed to protect him, not us," complained Julian, obviously scared.

Drew ignored his fear as he thought out loud. "The meeting is at three-thirty, that's an hour and eight minutes from now."

"Correct," answered Julian.

Still thinking out loud, Drew said, "I estimate Pat will arrive at the compound in about fifty minutes or so."

"Yes. But, Drew, I didn't anticipate so many cops, and snipers, no less. This is fucking dangerous."

"As I see it, Julian, the first problem is how do I get in before Pat arrives. I need to see things first hand."

Reluctantly, Julian offered, "There's that back fire road we talked about."

"Yeah. I could take that. It's actually much shorter than this road, and it leads right past the back of the ranch and its main house."

"Drew, the UAVs are the problem. You'll have to walk about a quarter mile. They will pick up your car for sure," Julian persisted.

"I can walk that. As I remember, you said there's plenty of tall sagebrush and pinyon pines along the way. Right?'

"Yes."

"Then that's it. We'll use the fire road. Once I'm in position, we'll decide what to do next."

"If you do this, Drew, it really complicates things. To abort, I will have to get Pat and Mario's guys and now you out without the cops or the Feds knowing. We're spread all over the place and can't support one another. We should go now."

"Calm down, Julian. We have the element of surprise and you have planned this well," Drew replied in a calm voice. "Trust me, Julian, we will all get out safely. Now, the two snipers. You got our guys behind them, right?"

"Yes."

"If we shoot them, that might alert the house," Drew thought out loud.

"Our men have scoped rifles with silencers," Julian reassured.

"Then that's the plan. If the snipers make a move on Pat, then kill them. I'll worry about the consequences later."

"We kill anyone then they will . . ."

Drew interrupted the panicking tech expert. "Look. Kill them if they make a hostile move. If not, our task is to get Pat safely into the house, tape the incriminating statements, and then pick off the snipers so we can safely exit. Just as you and I planned."

"Okay. I understand, the snipers have our guys trapped. Makes sense."

"Now tell everyone our solution for this last-minute obstacle."

"I'll text everybody."

"Julian, wait. I need the route to the fire road."

"Oh, of course." A minute later, he said, "Drew, turn around. The trail is about a thousand feet behind you. Take the small dirt road to your right. I've entered the route into your GPS. And, Drew, no hot dogging. The dust will draw the UAVs to you."

*Shit, what a mess. Julian is right. Everything is fucked up. But we can't run now.*

Drew turned the Beamer around and drove back to the fire road. Eighteen minutes later, he said, "Julian, let me know where I should pull over and go by foot."

"I've got you. Another two to three thousand feet. Park under the tall thicket of trees ahead."

Minutes later. "I'm here. How far ahead is the ranch?"

"Another ten minutes if you walk slow. You'll arrive a good twenty minutes before Pat."

Drew took off by foot as close as possible to the pine trees. He soon limped in behind a group of tall pinyons and a big outcropping of boulders, which overlooked the main house. "Julian, I'm here. Where is everyone?"

"Right here, Jefe."

Drew jumped. "Jesus, you scared me."

"You limp pretty bad. You okay?"

"Yeah, yeah. Mario, where is everyone?"

"Look at my laptop," Mario said, pointing to a satellite photo of the ranch. "Here's the driveway. Julio and Tio are behind the sniper on the eastside, here. Mark and Rodrigo are behind the one on the other side. Julian moved me so I could be with you."

"If I want to enter the house, how do I do it?"

"On the west side of the house is this side door to the garage, here. When I got here, it was unlocked."

"Now, Mario, where are our other men?"

"Here, Jefe," he said, pointing to an outcropping of large borders on the east side of the ranch house. "They are close enough to rush the front door quickly."

"The ones in the house, where are they?"

"Everyone seems to be on the first floor. Here, look at Julian's live video of the house." He changed the screen on his laptop. "Every once in a while they walk back and forth."

"So Julian can see them through the big glass window?"

"Sí. But, Jefe, if they're armed, it's really dangerous for us to rush the front door."

"How good are the guys behind the cop snipers?"

"Ex-army rangers. Julio is a decorated marksman. Afghanistan. Tio is his long-time spotter. Same for Mark and his spotter, Rodrigo. They know what they are doing. Drew, they're good."

"Did you tell them to shoot if it looks like Pat's in danger?"

"Julian texted them. I then asked if they could. They texted back, 'hell yes.' "

"Mario, I trust you. Pat's life is in your hands."

"No worry, Jefe. We owe our new lives to you. These pigs are going to die. One bad step and that's it. We with you man."

"I want to go inside. What's the best way?"

"Drew, why? You will tip them off. As soon as they see you, that's it."

"I need to be close to Pat so I can protect him."

"Jefe, the cops will kill Pat and you as soon as the two of you are together. Let us do it."

"You're too far back. I've got to be inside the house, close, say in the garage."

"But, Drew, if the door from the garage into house is locked!"

"I'll figure something out."

"Jefe, they intend to kill you. Look," Mario handed his infrared scope with an attached surveillance microphone to Drew. "We can listen in and see their body movements, even through walls. As soon as things get hot, we move. Here, use the earbuds. You can hear too."

Drew listened for a few minutes. "Those sons-of-bitches, they're saying how they will kill Pat as soon as he tells them what I know."

"See, I told you so."

"Are you recording this?"

"Sí. Julian and I both got every bit since we got here. These really bad people."

"Mario, if we take out the snipers, can Julio and Mark still shoot through the windows if things go bad?'

"We had them positioned to do that. That was how we cover our run to the door. But Julian moved them to the snipers."

"My question, Mario, is can they reposition immediately if needed?"

"I'll ask."

Mario texted the two teams. Both replied. Drew read the replies.

"Okay, they say no problem. This is what we're going to do. Let everyone know after Pat enters the house, the snipers are to be killed. Then have both teams move to a position where they can shoot into the house."

"Sí. That good. It will give us cover to rush the door."

"And, Mario, as soon as the snipers are neutralized, I'll move into the house if things get dangerous for Pat."

"Jefe . . ."

"No, Mario, it's settled."

"Sí."

Twenty minutes later, Drew called Julian on the burner phone. "Julian, where is Pat?"

"He just arrived. But he went past the driveway and pulled over into a tree-lined downhill runaway ramp. I see Feds there, about twenty or so. Armed to the teeth. Some look military. They got helmets, vests, M16s—the full gear. Pat's talking to them. Those UAVs got to be theirs."

"Any indication they know about us?"

"None so far. We got here well before them. I know 'cause I drove the road about a mile east and I was careful to check on the route up." Suddenly, Julian shouted into the mic, "Drew, they're spreading out and proceeding through the pines and sage toward the house."

"Who?"

"The Feds."

"Julian, tell our guys to stay low. And don't get shot. Give up their guns if confronted."

"Okay, Drew. Man this is more than I ever imagined. Drew, you said the Feds would just record Pat and the chief. This is a full scale raid."

"Julian, don't hang up."

Drew turned to his friend. "Mario, what do we do? Shoot the snipers before they see the Feds? Pat hasn't even entered the driveway."

"We gotta call it off, Jefe."

"No, not a good option." It took Drew just moments to figure out what to do. He pulled out his own cell phone, pushed the asterisk key, and punched is several numbers.

"Julian, stay on the burner while I call Mancini," Drew instructed.

"Mancini. Agent Mancini?"

"Drew, I don't have time. I'm busy," came the answer from the agent on the other end of the cell phone.

"Kiefer, I know exactly what you are doing. Your SWAT team is walking into an ambush, which will ruin the entire operation."

"What?"

"You heard me. Stop them now. And keep your UAVs away from the house."

"Where are you?"

"Watching the whole thing. There are two police snipers on either side of the driveway. Your guys are about thirty yards from being seen. Stop them now."

Drew heard Mancini yell, "Stop the tactical team. There are lookouts."

"Kiefer, there are three, maybe four in the house along with the two snipers. Send Pat in now. If he doesn't go down that driveway, they'll know something's wrong."

"Hawke, where are you?"

"Just listen, Kiefer. Once Pat's inside, I can take out the snipers. That way the ones in the house won't know you're here."

"God damn it, Hawke, don't tell me what to do."

"And elevate that tethered quad of yours higher so you can see the snipers."

"Drew," Julian shouted through the burner being held by Mario. "Tell him three thousand feet so the cops can't see it. Tell them to use its zoom camera . . . on the quad."

"Hawke, enough. Where . . ."

Drew interrupted. "The two snipers are about thirty yards in from the highway, about fifteen yards up the knoll on either side of the driveway. Make sure your SWAT guys stay well behind the knoll and away from the house."

"Shit. Frank, are you hearing this?" Kiefer said to his assistant.

"Got it. Moving the Orion up to three thousand feet." After a minute, Frank added, "Ah-hah, there they are. Kiefer, the kid is right."

"Damn it, Hawke, I will have your hide if this gets screwed up."

"Kiefer, I could give a shit."

# CHAPTER TWENTY-FOUR

Drew watched as a second quad circled high over the ranch compound.

"Julian, what are the Feds doing? There's a UAV circling above me."

"I imagine they are looking for us."

*God damn Kiefer.* Drew took out his cell phone and dialed again. He could tell there was someone on the other end. "Kiefer, quit stalling and send in Pat. It will do you no good looking for me."

"Don't tell me how to do my job, Hawke. Make this easy and call off your men."

"You know, Kiefer, I'm half tempted to shoot that quad down just to spite you."

"Don't you dare. That's government property."

"Then ground your UAV."

"Why should I?" came a voice behind Drew.

Drew swung about. "You sneaky son-of-a-bitch."

"You should talk, Hawke."

"Let's cut the crap, Kiefer. Don't worry about me and what I'm doing. Just send in Pat. We're running out of time," demanded Drew.

"You're obstructing the sting. And you are not shooting at anything. We can take out those snipers."

"Do you know where my snipers are?"

"Your snipers?

"Yeah."

"Ah . . . no."

"Then let's talk compromise. I will tell my guys not to shoot until you say so if you promise not to charge any of my men."

"They have to stand down," demanded Kiefer.

"Can't. They're already in place. Well hidden since early this morning. Your guys aren't. If your tactical team advances, you risk detection. Are you willing to risk the success of the operation?"

Kiefer looked at Drew with a blank expression. After a momentary pause, "I guess you have a point. Let's do a joint effort."

"Ooh-kay," Drew responded hesitantly.

Kiefer didn't wait for further demands. "First, who are the people in the house?"

"Chief James Shaughnessy and about three, possibly four other men. Probably cops. One of them I think is Detective Tom Clayton."

"Great, we got them all together. Now, Drew, where is everyone so my men don't shoot yours. We don't want anyone hurt in a crossfire."

Drew opened his laptop and showed the agent. "Our snipers are here. Three other of our men are here," he said, pointing to the outcropping of boulders near the front entrance to the house. "All our men are armed. The ones nearest the house will rush the door on my signal."

"And, how do you know what's going on inside the house. I don't see a drone."

"Infrared scope and parabolic listening equipment," Drew replied.

"Where is that?"

"Uh-uh, Kiefer. I need to know what you can see and hear."

"Fine, let's share intelligence so we both know what's going on inside."

"Agreed."

"Now, how did you know about this operation?"

"No can do. Mancini, that's not part of the bargain. Nor are the identity of any of my men and how we got our equipment."

"Damn you, Hawke . . ."

"Come on, Kiefer. Be cool. Remember, we both have the same objective. Let's keep it at that. Okay?" Kiefer appeared about to explode. His face was beet red as he clenched his teeth.

"Agent Mancini, we can do this. I put away my ego and you do what's best for us all. Oly baby will praise you for making the right decision."

"Don't try buttering my ass, Hawke. Wyland will crucify me for not knowing what you were up to."

"That's not the way to begin our courtship, Kiefer. We'll deal with Oly later. Let's get those bastards."

Mancini pushed the microphone underneath his FBI jacket. "Frank."

"Yes, Kiefer."

"You need to talk to Drew. We have to hook up our intel with his. He's got infrared and audio surveillance into the house. If it's good, figure out a way to coordinate our system with what they got. Tell swat to stay hidden until I say advance. Tell them there are friendlies surrounding the house. They're Drew's damn guys. They have guns but will not shoot. I need your recommendation on how to advance once you view where Drew's men are and you see their intel. Tell Pat what's going on and that Drew is already here, and, well, hasn't screwed anything up yet."

"Yes, sir."

Drew leaned close to Kiefer's lapel mic. "Frank, we got to get Pat in the house within ten minutes or everything is screwed." As Drew stepped back he noticed Kiefer's expression. *Oops, I don't think Kiefer appreciated my suggestion.*

Mario tapped Drew on the shoulder and whispered in his ear. "Jefe, you shouldn't piss the man off. They Feds."

Drew took the burner phone from Mario and called Julian. "Hey, Mancini is with me. He's agreed to share what we see with the intel the Feds have from the drones and whatever." Turning to Mancini, he added, "Right, Kiefer?"

"Yes," the agent said into the phone.

"So without mentioning any names or exposing your electronic hacks and how you did it, please cooperate fully with them."

Drew listened to his tech wizard's recommendation. He turned to Mancini. "How do you and Frank communicate?"

"Through FBI satellites."

"Figured so. Here's our laptop. Call Frank and figure out how to connect our system with yours. Let's connect Frank and Julian together and let them do their thing."

After about ten precious minutes, with Frank telling Julian how to hook into an FBI satellite, the two started connecting UAV surveillance to the civilian equipment Mario and Julian were using.

"Look, Kiefer." Drew lifted Mario's laptop and showed the three segmented images displayed on the screen.

Mancini seemed impressed with the combined surveillance. Drew proceeded to suggest a plan of action. The agent seemed to approve the plan of action until . . .

"Kiefer, I suggest once Pat drives in and enters the house, I slip into the garage through that side door." He pointed to the door on the screen. "You stay here and command operations. I'm putting Pat's and my own life in your hands. Here's what we've heard so far—as soon as the cops learn what I know, they intend to kill Pat and, if I'm caught, me, of course."

"I'd prefer you stay out of the house."

"Thank you, Kiefer. I appreciate that. But I have to be able to announce my presence in order to give you time to charge the house before they kill either one of us. Otherwise, they may just shoot Pat once he says I don't know anything about the covered-up shooting or the Enforcers. I know Pat. This is exactly what he'll say, thinking he is protecting me."

With a somewhat smirk, Mancini said, "So you propose to be the bait that provides time for us to act?"

"Yes. Otherwise they will kill Pat as soon as they know we're outside."

A few moments later, Pat's car entered the driveway and proceeded up to the house. Julian reported he observed one of the snipers phoning someone. Then both snipers turned so they had a shot at the house.

Mancini whispered to Drew, "They're smart. They plan to kill Pat as he drives away. They know if they shoot him inside, there's no guarantee they can completely clean that house."

"That police chief is just covering his ass," Drew replied.

"If that is the plan, then you don't go in."

"Sorry, Kiefer. To be safe I have to be close enough to act, just in case. I'll stay in the garage until Pat is out."

Mancini agreed, but Drew knew what he would do if anything went wrong.

Pat knocked on the ranch door. A young man pulled the door open, "Are you Pat De Luca?"

"Yes."

As Drew listened, the greeter's voice sounded familiar but Drew couldn't place it.

"I'm here to see Chief James Shaughnessy."

"That's Pat," Drew said.

"Shush," ordered Mancini.

"And who might you be," asked Pat.

"Luke, sir. Luke D'Angelo."

"Oh. Didn't you fight Drew?"

"Yes, sir."

A second voice was heard. "Come on in, Pat."

Drew held the burner phone to his lips and whispered, "Pat's in the house."

"What did you say?" demanded Kiefer.

"Tell you later. I have to get in there. Drew ran bent low toward the garage door.

"Mario, he's limping. Something wrong with Drew?" Mancini asked.

"I think his burnt feet hurt."

Mancini pushed the button on his body mic. "Frank, Operation Canary is in effect. Pat's in the house. Canary is a go."

"Got it, Kiefer," came the reply.

Mario looked at the agent. "What's canary?"

Kiefer ignored the question. Mario started to ask again but saw Drew grab the door handle. Just as he predicted, the door was unlocked.

Once inside Drew, quietly moved to the door into the main house and leaned forward to listen.

Drew texted Mario. 'Turn up the audio, can't hear."

Mario replied with thumbs-up emoji as Hawke put the ear buds back into his ears.

"I think you know everybody, Tony MacNeal and Tom Clayton."

Drew listen with a shocked look upon hearing MacNeal's name."

"Check him for a gun," came an order.

*That's got to be James Shaughnessy*, thought Drew.

"Yeah, and a mic," another voice added.

"I'm clean, Clayton," Pat replied.

"He's right, Chief. Nothing," reassured the third male voice.

*That's got to be Tony,* Drew surmised.

"Gentlemen, thanks for meeting." *That's Pat.* "I didn't know, Tony, you were an Enforcer."

"Wow," said Drew out loud at the thought of Tony, a life-long friend, being an Enforcer.

"De Luca, you asked for the meeting," Shaughnessy stated.

"Chief, why the attack on Drew?"

"It was to be a message only. We didn't know he was on board—"

"Don't play coy, De Luca," Detective Clayton interrupted before the chief could finish.

"Tom, back off," replied Pat.

"Calm down, you two."

"Chief, why involve Drew in any of this?" Pat asked again.

"I don't think we have to answer any questions, De Luca," Clayton stated.

"Oh yes you do. Why stir up this twenty-year-old mess and target a kid I've help raise?"

"Okay, you two, I said enough," Shaughnessy said, raising his voice.

"What we want to know is why does Hawke represent Carlos Guerra, the last of the Mexicans involved in the carjack?"

"He doesn't any longer. The fire crippled him. He gave the case to another attorney who handles federal court matters. And, he knows nothing about the Enforcers."

"What does he know about the De Jesus brothers?"

"Nothing, Chief. He doesn't know Tom killed Juan De Jesus. I've kept the code."

"See? I told you, Chief, Pat knows. Answer the question," demanded Clayton. "Quit fucking around. What does Hawke know?"

"Damn it, Tom, I'm getting pretty tired of your constant interruptions."

"Stop it, you two. What I want to know is why did Hawke take the Guerra case?"

"Chief, he didn't know its history. He still doesn't. Carlos Guerra is just another client that showed up at his door. Drew doesn't even know I was involved or how things went down twenty years ago."

"You haven't told him?"

"No, Tom. Nor do I intend to."

"That would be smart."

"Tom, I'm going to ignore that threat. Chief, I lived by the code as an officer even though I wasn't one of the Enforcers. And I will keep silent until I die. It's how we live. The brotherhood can't exist without the code. How else can we survive. The assholes we fight want to kill us."

"You talk the talk, De Luca, but I don't believe it."

"Clayton . . ." Pat paused for a moment. "I backed your ass for years. Nearly got killed getting us out of the stupid shit you pulled. Stuff a cop shouldn't do. So don't shit on me now. I was a good partner for years, even though I didn't agree with what you did."

"Stop it! Stop, you two," demanded Chief Shaughnessy.

"You fight like an old married couple. What either of you did in the past is the past. The problem is Hawke. He's a dangerous lawyer. He has caused the judge and us a lot of problems."

"That he has," added Detective Clayton.

"Who's us, the Enforcers?" queried Pat.

"No," injected Clayton.

"Shut up, you fool," ordered the chief.

"Jesus, Chief, a 'fool.' You don't have say it that way," pleaded Clayton.

"It is what it is, Tom. You've made some really bad choices. We wouldn't be here if you hadn't overreacted and shot them."

"But, Chief . . ."

"Damn it, Tom, you knew they weren't armed. What you did long ago can take us all down, and the judge won't like that."

"Chief, I admit I didn't think, but I fixed everything by taking care of Manny."

"You did what? Clayton are you saying you're responsible for the death of Manny, too?" Pat shouted.

"Pat, fuck you. He was talking stupid shit about me in prison. He got what he deserved."

"I can't believe this. Chief, Tom has to stop. First Juan De Jesus, then Manny. And now Hawke. Enough is enough. Look, guys, I'll make sure Drew stays out of the Guerra case. What happens after that is Clayton's problem."

"You hanging me out to dry, Pat? Is that where we are? Huh?"

"Calm down, Tom. Nobody is abandoning you," the chief said in an effort to sooth the detective. "If Pat says he will keep Hawke out of the Guerra case then what's the beef with the kid?"

"He's a pain in the ass, Chief."

Drew laughed out loud as he listened.

"Chief," injected Pat, "the fact that Drew makes a fool out of Tom doesn't justify killing the boy. If Tom keeps this up, we're all going to be in trouble."

"Trouble? Who's going to get into trouble? You threatening me, De Luca? What happened to the code," spewed Clayton.

"You know, Tom, you blurt shit before you think," Pat attacked back but quickly added in a calm voice, "Tom, you don't kill a prominent attorney, especially one as popular as Hawke. People will demand a thorough investigation."

"Tom, settle down. Pat has a point. We don't want the DA or even the FBI snooping around. Let the judge take care of the kid. There's no reason to bring any heat on us."

"I don't think so, Chief," the red-faced detective replied, glaring at Pat.

"Then it's agreed. I keep Drew away from the Guerra case and you don't try anything else against him. Right, Chief?"

"Bullshit deal," shouted Clayton. "It's my ass that's on the line. I want more."

"What the fuck," shouted Pat as Clayton pulled his Glock.

"Put the gun away," Shaughnessy ordered.

"No way. Chief, there can't be any loose ends."

"Kill! Kill," Drew whispered into the burner as he pushed the door open and stepped into the room.

"Hawke!" Clayton growled. "I told you, Chief, they're in cahoots. Pat's been lying all along."

"As usual, Clayton, you have your head up your ass," Drew drawled with a sarcastic smile as he walked past D'Angelo and stood in front of the cabin's large front window, causing the detective to turn away from De Luca.

"Pat didn't know I followed him. And, he's right. I no longer represent Guerra."

"You lie, Hawke," the thoroughly out of control man yelled.

"Put that gun down and say that to my face. You've been wanting to kick my ass forever."

"You're a dead man," Clayton yelled as he raised the gun toward the attorney.

"Clayton, the code, remember the Blue Code. Shooting Drew violates how we treat one another and our close friends," screamed Pat.

"He's right, Tom," joined the chief. Put the damn gun down. Not here."

"No way, Chief," Clayton replied as he walked forward and took aim.

"No," shouted Luke D'Angelo as he stepped in front of Drew. "I didn't come here for . . ."

But the infuriated detective fired, striking D'Angelo square in the chest.

"You son-of-a-bitch. Why did you shoot him? You're an animal. Look at me. You want to kill me? Here I am," Drew shouted, his arms outstretched. "Unarmed, the way a coward likes to kill. Shoot, you selfish dick!"

"Tom, you flinch and I will blow your head off," a voice shouted from behind Clayton.

Clayton slowly looked to his left and slightly behind him. Drew sensed a chance to strike but hesitated as Clayton's eyes glanced back.

"You, too, Tony," Clayton yelled looking at Drew. "You're in this with De Luca. You and Pat?"

"Yes, and I will kill you if you shoot Hawke. Put the gun down. *Now!*"

A slight swish of air brushed right to left across the front of Drew's head, followed by a slow-motion image of Clayton's left frontal skull beginning to separate into tiny fragments of flesh, bone, and a grayish white matter. Glass could be heard falling to the floor. Drew felt stinging sensations and a warm moisture against his face as Clayton's head moved in segmented images to the man's right. With time morphed into apparent aminated suspension, a second separation appeared at the back of Clayton's head, followed instantaneously by the sound of an explosion from behind the detective. Drew watched, mesmerized by the slow disintegration of Clayton's brain as human flesh flew everywhere. A thick substance slid down Hawke's face.

The loud blast of the shot reverberated throughout the room. Drew just stood, deafened, while all hell erupted about him. The only thing that registered was Clayton's body slumping down out of sight.

Drew stood motionless, smeared with blood and flesh. The front door was kicked in and a flood of people rushed in. After a moment or two, Drew heard a distinct sound, a voice that grew louder. Drew's mind raced as he tried to make sense of what just happened and the events swirling about him. He heard a familiar sound as a hand touched him. He spun away instinctively with fists raised as preservation took over.

"Drew, son, are you all right? Speak to me, boy, it's Pat."

# CHAPTER TWENTY-FIVE

**Several weeks later**

Five men made their way through the San Diego County Court House. As they exited the elevators, everyone in the crowded hallway turned and looked at the man being pushed in a wheelchair and the blue raid jackets worn by three of the men. The jackets had printed badges on the front and U.S. Marshal emblazoned across the back in bold, white letters. The fifth man, wearing a suit, opened the door so the party could enter the courtroom of the Presiding Judge of the San Diego County Superior Courts. The deputy sheriff immediately rose from his desk.

"It's okay, Deputy Stout. We're here to see Judge O'Shea," Drew said as one of the marshals walked over and stood next to the deputy.

The deputy, with a stunned look, watched as the men went to the open door leading into the hallway to the judge's chamber. Drew pushed himself up from the wheelchair while Agent Mancini handed him a pair of crutches.

"Wait here, Kiefer. I want to talk to my father alone."

Drew carefully hobbled his way to Brian O'Shea's chamber. Drew pushed the door open with a crutch and defiantly looked at the robed judge seated behind his desk.

"I didn't know you had a standing invitation to walk into my chambers at any time."

"And just because you fathered me doesn't mean you have a right to constantly interfere in my life," came the challenge back.

"You are indeed a feisty one today. Did the fire bring out the courage to confront me or was it the arrest of Shaughnessy?"

"You son-of-a-bitch. You were in on the attempt to kill me."

"Drew, I would never bring any harm to you. You are my son. So get off your high horse," the man said as he lifted his huge frame from his chair and walked around the desk.

Drew immediately dropped his crutches and readied to fight.

"Relax, boy. I love you. Hit me if you must, but I will not fight back."

"You cowardly bastard. You are a crook who steals from the public treasury. A disgrace to the robe and the law you swore to uphold."

"You done venting?"

"No. The FBI knows all about you, Shaughnessy, the mayor, and the money you've hidden in the Cayman Islands."

"I don't know what you're talking about, Drew. I hear the Feds raided some Caribbean bank and found nothing."

"They're tracing the money now. They'll find where you've hidden it. Then you're done."

"You seem so confident about my involvement in this police scandal. Hear my words clearly. I had nothing to do with those crooks. And, if and when they find any money, I want you to crawl in here and apologize."

"That will be a cold day in hell . . . father."

"All right, you want it out, let's do it. You are so consumed with hatred you just can't give me a chance. Yes, I screwed up.

Yes, you had a right to know who I was. And, yes, I should have been there for you. But your mother demanded I stay away."

"That's because she knew exactly what you are."

"Whatever she thought of me does not mean I don't deserve a chance to make things up to you."

Drew just stood there, not knowing what to say.

"Drew, you've grown into an upstanding man. Not afraid to take the world on. I see a lot of me in you. A hard driving, ambitious lawyer."

"I'm not anything like you," protested Drew.

"Oh yes you are. More than you'll ever realize. You got my genes. My intelligence. My physical gifts, which I must say you sportingly use to your advantage."

"Bullshit."

"That's not what Judith says."

"You dick, always meddling in my life. Sending Judge Hudson to have sex with me. You're just playing with my personal feelings and Judith's. You're a sadistic man. You're willing do anything to control me. It's over—now and forever."

"You can't shut me out, Drew. I'm part of you. Always you will wonder what part is exactly like me."

"Nothing," Drew stammered. "I'm not going to be like you."

"Boy, you're young, idealistic. That's how youth are, especially after law school. Full of principles, rosy ideas about justice and the rights of man."

Drew was stunned by the formidable man in front of him. *I've got to get the conversation off of me and back to the kickback scheme.*

"What's wrong with being who I am?" asked Hawke.

"You will learn, son, life is not the naive way you think."

"How is it, father," he replied with a sarcastic challenge.

"You may doubt my words, but the law grants us power. A

power that serves mostly the wealthy. Money buys power and power is money. Here they all meet in my courthouse. I decide how justice is served and to whom power is shared."

"You're sick, father." Drew paused to let the words sink in. "You're consumed with power and by power. Don't you see that? That's why you got sucked in by Mayfield, Sandleson, and Shaughnessy."

"Come now, you are over reacting. Think about what I say. Look around you. Son, open your eyes to reality. If you do, you will learn how to grasp the golden ring on this merry-go-round of life. Drew, law is your tool. Use it to grab power and money. Come, let me share it with you," the judge said, extending his hand.

"Stop. I am ashamed to say your blood runs in my veins. That your genes are part of me. Brian O'Shea, you are a sick man." His voice quivered as his words trailed off.

"Kiefer, get in here," Drew shouted.

The agent and the two marshals walked in.

"Brian O'Shea, you have been implicated in a series of crimes . . ." Mancini began.

"Careful, Mr. FBI. Watch what you say and what you do. I had a long telephone talk this morning with Oly Wyland. We discussed the corruption in the police department and the rumors about one of my judges being involved. I assured him I would fully cooperate and would meet with you for an interview. Have a seat, Kiefer Mancini," the judge directed, pointing to a chair in front of his desk.

"Mr. Hawke, you will pick up your crutches and wait in my courtroom while I talk to these federal officers alone," the judge ordered as he swung about, his black robe flaring out as he moved to his chair.

Drew looked at Mancini. The agent picked up the crutches. "Here, wait outside, Drew."

Once seated, the judge looked contemptuously at Hawke.

"Go ahead, Drew, wait outside," Mancini said in a calm voice. "Marshal Veach, help Mr. Hawke to the courtroom."

Twenty-five minutes later, Mancini, followed by a marshal, walked into the courtroom. "Drew, let's go."

"What'd he say? You going to arrest him?"

"Let's talk back at your office."

ooooo

On crutches, Drew pushed open the door and entered his law office, followed by Mancini. Debbie, Liz, and Matt immediately stood.

Drew looked at them and headed toward his office. He stopped at the doorway and turned around. "Debbie, please hold all my calls."

With the door closed, he said, "Okay, we're here. So let's hear it, Kiefer, what did he say?" Catching his rude voice and defiant posture, Drew added, "Oh, sorry, have a seat."

Once the agent was seated, Drew noticed the agent's expression—it wasn't encouraging.

"It was just a regurgitation of what he told Wyland," the agent said.

"And?"

"Without a paper trail showing he's connected to the money or where he has hidden it, we just don't have enough evidence to arrest. In fact, there really isn't anything showing the mayor or O'Shea were involved in a kickback scheme or that they were involved with the Enforcers."

"What about Shaughnessy? Doesn't he implicate O'Shea in something?"

"So far he won't say O'Shea is part of the influence peddling or that O'Shea knew about the rogue cops."

"How about the Cayman bank accounts?"

"A well-paid Cayman lawyer set up those corporate bank accounts. Not O'Shea. The lawyer was the sole signatory on those accounts. The bank records showed the attorney was given signing power to distribute money, even close the accounts, which is exactly what he did."

"Kiefer, you've got Mayfield and Sandleson signing corporate resolutions authorizing the opening of those accounts."

"True."

"Such a document of authorization or a corporate power of attorney for the Cayman lawyer to act should be enough to prosecute . . ." Drew continued to argue only to be interrupted.

"Drew, the fact is O'Shea insulated himself with Sandleson, Morgan, and the Cayman lawyer."

"But such acts are circumstantial evidence . . ." Drew paused as he realized he was arguing details and potential legal theories that were not the best evidence or even enough to bring a possible winning case.

"So he's used them as shields!"

"Yes. The powerful always have an intermediary. He even had Shaughnessy between him and the Enforcers. Nothing traces back to the judge."

Recognizing the defeat, Drew slumped back in his chair.

"Unless someone talks, the FBI can't get to Brian O'Shea," Kiefer finally admitted.

"My father was correct. Power is money. Money buys silence and corruption wins. All this was a bust? Risking Pat's life, mine, even endangering my staff was all for naught."

The young lawyer paused, and, in a low whisper, he added, "Nearly killing Mia . . . now losing her forever." Hawke glared at Mancini. "And what about D'Angelo? One of the good cops. I want to see him so I can thank him for saving my life."

The agent shook his head. "He's in a coma. He had on a bullet-proof vest, but at that close range, he still suffered a fractured sternum and bruised heart. He's unlikely to ever cage fight again, and he may not be able to return to active duty."

In an angry outburst, Drew shouted, "And all we got was a police chief and few dirty cops."

"I wouldn't go that far. The case is still open," Mancini said. "The fact Shaughnessy confirms our suspicions about the Enforcers, and even the existence of a corrupt judge, means we're on the right track. We just have to figure out how these people used their positions of power to steal money. If we find the money, we'll know how much, and then we can trace it back to specific dates of the action they took."

"Yes, yes, I know, the money has been filtered through too many hands for you to know anything of substance right now?"

"Yes. But, Drew, it's impossible to hide the transfer of money. We will eventually track it down. Sooner or later they will make a mistake."

Drew looked at the man with a wary smile, provoking Kiefer to reassure him.

"The government never stops. We will find the evidence necessary to get them."

"Not too comforting, Kiefer. What about Mayfield?"

"The publicity has ended his business life. We indicted him, but couldn't proceed without the money. We just can't connect his projects to influence peddling without the money. Oly had to offer him a plea deal based on his apparent efforts to hide money overseas. Because we were able to show money left his New

Jersey company and was never reported as income to the IRS, he's agreed to plead to tax fraud. He will serve three years and have to pay a fine of six million."

"Six million," growled Drew. "What was that figure based on?"

"The amount of money that we could prove went offshore through his corporation and wasn't reported. There will be heavy penalties and interest added, so it will be a heavy hit. His ability to do business is ended."

"Funny how crooked money works. Nobody really ever rots in jail. The only real hurt is a hit to their wallet." The young lawyer sighed. The two sat silent as Drew held a cynical look at the federal agent.

Finally Mancini spoke. "Drew, I appreciate your willingness to work with us. And you even tried to provoke an incriminating statement out of O'Shea. I know that was a difficult moment for you. I mean to hear what type of a man he is. He was just too smart to take the bait. I'm afraid O'Shea knows what he's doing."

"This isn't the end of this," Drew said. "I can at least expose how he sexually abused female court employees—my mother. That might even force him to resign."

"Think about what you do," the agent cautioned. "It may affect our ultimate ability to arrest him. We could reach a dead end if he resigns and goes off to some place far away."

"Kiefer, are you saying out of sight out of mind?"

"Not exactly. Remember, the best made plans of crooks have a way of unraveling over time as we pick off one crook after another."

Mancini stood. "Drew, I sincerely admire how you risked your life for those you love and the great effort you made to help us. I know it was gut wrenching to learn about O'Shea and the corruption we are investigating. If you need anything in the future, call."

The two shook hands and Mancini left.

# CHAPTER TWENTY-SIX

The gray-haired priest in his black cassock strode with purpose down the hall from his rectory. It was well past the time to lock the doors of the cathedral. He had fallen asleep reading about the death of Saint Ignatius of Antioch.

Still contemplating the last words of the saint, Father Joseph O'Connor was oblivious to his surroundings as he exited the vestry and walked to the center of the sanctuary. He stopped, turned toward the alter, knelt, and blessed himself. As he turned and walked down the center aisle of the cathedral's dark nave, the faint figure of a body in gray sweatpants and a hoodie lying on a pew began to appear.

Once near, the priest slowed but couldn't tell if it was a soul in emotional distress or someone seeking shelter from the damp cold night. Father O'Connor quietly stepped into the pew and knelt about four feet away. The priest blessed himself and began praying.

Nearly ten-minutes passed as the priest prayed for the troubled person lying next to him. Slowly, the body stirred and then sat up. The man brushed back his hoodie. The priest looked startled as he recognized who it was.

"What troubles you, son?"

"Father," came the response as the surprised young man looked to his left.

"You are a little early for confession. We don't start until seven tomorrow evening."

"Sorry, Father, I got lost in my thoughts and dozed off."

The priest straightened up and sat on the pew. "May I sit with you?"

"Of course. What time is it?"

The priest glanced at his watch. "It's eleven-ten."

"Oh, my. I've been asleep a while."

"Not to worry. You obviously needed to rest. I see things have been quite traumatic for you these past weeks."

"Traumatic doesn't really describe my life lately. I came to talk with you but couldn't really find the right way to ask for your advice. I just don't know what to do about everything that's happened."

"Now is as good a time as any. Why not start with what bothers you most."

"My father. The judge."

"So you know?"

"Yes. I confronted him. I went to his chambers and told him I knew about him being part of the corruption plaguing the police and the city."

"And?"

"He accused me of hating him because he abandoned me."

"Do you?"

Drew looked away, then directly at Father O'Connor. "Damn it. Yes, I do," he said in a loud, angry tone. His words echoed in the empty cathedral.

"Why?" the priest asked, sensing the man he baptized and has counseled since a small boy was at a crisis point in his life.

"I don't know. That's why I've been here all night. I just don't know why I hate him so. Yes, he's a crook, but I don't think that's all of it."

The priest said nothing. His silence begged more.

Finally, Drew continued. "Father, the bastard denied

everything. No matter how many times I told him the FBI knew everything about him, the mayor, and police chief, he just kept denying it all. He said my anger about him is why I believe what they say."

"Do you want to believe him?"

"I can't. There's too much evidence."

"But . . ." the priest paused, choosing his words carefully. "But do you want to believe him."

"Yes, of course. Who wants a father who is a thief, a con-artist. A man who uses his power to take."

"I see."

"Father O'Connor, I always wanted to know about him. But Mom, Pat, and Lauren all said he died right after I was born. That was a lie. Even you deceived me."

"Drew, I never said your father was dead. Are we talking about who your father is or that the truth was hidden from you?"

"I understand why Mom hid the truth from me. He isn't the type of man anyone would want as a father."

"Are you sure that is the sole reason? You and I have known each other a long time. This isn't the first time we've talked about Judge O'Shea. That man has meddled in your life and your practice for years."

"Father, he begged me to let him be a part of my life. The bastard even asked me to join him. Use the law to gain power and money. I almost threw up right in front of him."

"Are you tempted to join him?"

"No. O'Shea stands for everything I loathe. He is the evil that the law opposes, that the law is supposed to eliminate. And yet . . ." The lawyer went silent and once again turned away.

"And yet what?"

"I don't know . . . I don't know what's worse, the power of the government or those who wield that power for their own purposes."

The priest said nothing as he watched the lawyer struggle with what appeared to be his purpose in law, even his long-held personal beliefs.

"Father O'Connor, I am convinced power corrupts. Just as it has corrupted my father. I can't help but think he . . . he didn't start out this way. What happened to him? He said his blood runs through my body. He is part of me."

Nothing was said by either man. Hawke looked down as if fearful of what might be said next. The elderly man seemed to be at a loss for an answer.

"So, Drew . . ." He paused until Hawke looked at him. "Does the fact that part of you came from him mean you will become another Brian O'Shea?"

"God help me. Yes."

Silence once again filled the cathedral. The shear absence of sound seemed to scream at the two.

Slowly, the priest spoke, "I fell asleep reading about Saint Ignatius." He paused as if knowing each word must be chosen carefully. Moments passed and yet the gray-haired man just sat there.

Drew looked at him with a sense of bewilderment. *Why is he talking about falling asleep?* He screamed inside himself, *Help me, Father O'Connor. What do I do about O'Shea?*

"Yes, I think there is meaning in how Saint Ignatius of Antioch died," the priest continued. "Ignatius was an early Christian writer. His letters are part of the evolution of Christian theology. He specifically addressed ecclesiology, the sacraments, and the role of bishops."

Frustrated, Drew interrupted. "Father O'Connor, I know

about Ignatius and the influence he had on the church and its role in the forgiveness of sin," Drew blurted out. "If you are telling me to forgive O'Shea, I will not do so."

"What I was about to say is that the Lord gave us humans a free will. A free will which can do good as well as harm. Saint Ignatius and other early Christian writers wrote about the role of the church in helping mankind recognize good from evil and then shine a path forward through repentance and the forgiveness of our sins."

"You're saying I don't have to be like O'Shea."

"If you so choose. The fact that you recognize the things Brian has done are wrong gives you a choice: To be like him or to choose another path. One that does good. You see, Drew, Saint Ignatius faced death when he wrote some of his most important letters. His Christian faith and position within the Church are why the Romans condemned him to death. Knowing he could be fed to the lions in the Colosseum, he still refused to deny Christ. Are you capable of . . ."

Again the lawyer interrupted. "Of knowing what I believe . . . is right . . . of not giving in to evil as my father has? Is that what you're asking?" Hawke snapped as he glared at the priest.

"Isn't that why you came here tonight?"

Drew slumped back into the pew. "Yes, I suppose it is. I'm afraid. What do I do?"

"We all recognize what is evil before we give in to it. It's easy to condemn evil, even to condemn it in the name of the Lord. But it is very hard to resist its temptations. Drew, those police officers started out to do their sworn duty. But somewhere along the way, whether for expediency's sake or just to get even, they did evil to fight evil. Once one does, the temptation to do other wrongs becomes strong. As does the lure of easy money."

"Do you think that's what happened to my father?"

"Brian O'Shea failed to resist the temptation of power and its companion greed. Yes, you are right. Power corrupts . . . if you allow it. Your challenge is to use your knowledge of the law and the powers of persuasion God gave you to do good."

"But what does that mean?"

"It means many things to many people. I as a priest believe good is achieved through the law when we understand why humans do horrible things. Not an easy task. But if you can understand human nature and why it does what it does, then you must somehow find a way through the law to rehabilitate such fallen souls so they may rejoin society and contribute to the good of all. But, Drew, not all people believe the way the Church does."

"Are you telling me I should try to save my father?"

"I think such a task is more in my realm. Brian and I go back decades, and we know each other very well. He understands what he has done and its consequences."

"But O'Shea must be stopped."

"You said the authorities are onto Brian, right?"

"Yes."

"Then why not leave Brian O'Shea to them. Then the priest added, "Remember, Drew, vengeance is all consuming—both emotionally and physically. You will realize this the older you get. Forgiveness is a power that prolongs life; hatred, even for a good reason, is a force that shortens life. Use your time to do good."

"I can't forgive him. Not unless he admits what he has done is wrong. And that he must face the consequences of those unlawful acts," Drew said in a raised voice. He stood as if to leave.

"Drew, please sit. Just a little longer."

"Fine," came a defiant reply as Drew sat.

"You have come to me since you were a boy. I have never told you what to do. Always my admonition to you has been be true to yourself. Do what you are capable of doing and what is best for you, and what was best for your mom when she was alive."

"O'Shea ruined my mother's life, and now he's ruining mine."

"Drew, your life hasn't been ruined. However, your choices going forth—those will decide what kind of a life you will have."

The priest shifted closer to the lawyer. He reached out and touched his arm. "Tell me the latest about Shaughnessy, the mayor, and that Mayfield guy. I hear the mayor is trailing in the polls as he fights for his reelection."

"Yes, the media and press have questioned every aspect of Mayor Sandleson's actions and criticized his choice of Shaughnessy as police chief. But the mayor continually states he knew nothing about the Enforcers or the police chief's involvement. He even points out how his insistence on good neighborhood policing has changed the police department. But the public seems ready to clean house both at city hall as well as in the police department."

"And the Enforcers? Are they still a threat . . . to you?"

"The FBI is striking deals with one Enforcer cop after another in exchange for information on who is involved. Agent Mancini seems to feel they will get most of the Enforcers, at least the ones who have kept the corrupt gang together all these years."

"But, your safety . . ."

Drew interrupted. "Oh, I guess I will never be totally safe. No one can guarantee some pissed-off cop won't want to teach me a lesson, but U.S. Attorney Wyland and Mancini feel Pat and Lauren and my office staff should be okay once all the prosecutions are over."

"And that young lady who was burned when your boat was attacked?"

"That's another matter. I guess I will never see her again."

"That's a shame. So you have many reasons to want revenge?"

"Oh, Father, yes I do."

"Thank you for sharing this with me. I understand better your anger and your desire for Brian to answer for his actions. But for now, why don't you think about what we've discussed. You have some serious decisions to make."

Drew nodded as he stood and offered his hand to the priest. The priest grasped Drew's hand in both of his own.

"Bless you, son. I'll pray that you make the right decisions as you deal with your father and all the challenges you face going forth. But remember this, Drew: You are a gifted young lawyer and the Lord has a plan on how you are to use those gifts for the good of mankind. May you always make the right decisions on how you live your life." The priest paused and with a smile added, "Will I see you soon at confession?"

Drew smiled back. "Of course."

# EPILOGUE

Month after month slowly passed as Drew Hawke resumed his life. The burns of the flesh healed but not the emotional scars. The mind is strange. It can handle such mortal things as burns all over one's body, but losing a loved one, that's different.

Little things bring back seemingly forgotten moments. Seeing Klimt's Woman in Gold, hearing Beethoven's Romance for violin, or a similar woman's voice, even the tilt of her head, is enough to cause a man to pause. Sometimes it can even be a wife's smile that creates a flood of emotions as memories of a long ago heartache flush uncontrollably forth. They say time heals such tormenting wounds. The real truth is: What happens to a loved one is never forgotten.

Over and over again the healing attorney told himself it was best that Mia was out of danger. Drew was too well known and his high profile trials had the press, even the paparazzi, following his every move. There was no way he could ever make any attempt to find her. The attorney thanked agent Mancini numerous times for coming up with the story she succumbed to her fire-seared lungs while secretly putting her into a federal protection program. That was the only way to protect her, even if it meant the young lawyer would never see her again.

Drew Hawke also appreciated the nearly five years of extended protection provided to Lauren and Pat, Debbie, and the law firm's employees. Oly Wyland was right—the best way to get revenge against Hawke and De Luca would be through those closest to them. The firing of the Artful Dodger and its lingering scars were a constant reminder no one would be safe until all the Enforcers were finally rooted out.

# ACKNOWLEDGEMENTS

In the further adventures of A.J. Hawke, a work of this intensity and technical detail would not be possible without the assistance of others, whom I wish to thank with my sincerest gratitude.

The cyber-security experts who helped me get the technical aspects of electronic surveillance correct. Thank you, gentlemen.

The priests who took time out of their busy schedules to help me research Saint Ignatius of Antioch. Their assistance has been most helpful.

My editor, Larry M. Edwards, without whom this manuscript would not have become a reality. Mr. Edwards, an award-winning author in his own right, has guided me through the plot twists and rewrites with a tremendous degree of patience and perseverance. Thank you, Larry.

Timothy Brittain, whose skills as a graphic artist extraordinaire again created an awesome cover design and page layout.

And to my readers, thank you for your enthusiastic interest in the A.J. Hawke series. I hope you find these books not only interesting because of their unique legal issues but also enlightening with regard to the many challenges lawyers face as they perform their role in our system of justice.

# A. J. Hawke Returns

Look for the next challenge A.J. Hawke faces as he comes to grips with the reality of life and how the law addresses the actions and needs of its citizens.

# About the Author

**Donald E. McInnis** is a California litiga-
tion attorney and the author of the fictional legal thriller series A.J. Hawke, Attorney at Law. Hawke is a young defense
attorney practicing law in the Gaslamp
Quarter of San Diego, California, where
he finds himself embroiled in cases involving murder and power politics.

Early in his career, Mr. McInnis
served as a Research Attorney for the California Superior
Courts. Later he became a Deputy District Attorney for two
different counties in Northern California and a Deputy Public
Defender in San Diego County.

He has also served as a Superior Court Judge Pro Tem, has
been an arbitrator for the American Arbitration Association,
and a referee/arbitrator for the California Superior Courts.

## Books
- She's So Cold: *The Stephanie Crowe Murder Case—A Defense
  Attorney's Inside Story* (true crime)
- *The Sphynx Murder Case—A.J. Hawke, Attorney at Law* (fiction)
- *Return of The Sphynx—An A.J. Hawke Legal Thriller* (fiction)
- *Blood of the Father – An A.J. Hawke Legal Thriller* (fiction)
- *Cops Gone Bad – An A.J. Hawke Legal Thriller* (fiction)

**LEGAL TREATISES:**

**The Initiative Process:**

*Money & Politics*, Citizens Initiative: Who Shall Govern, Santa Clara University Law Review, Volume 59, Issue 1, Fall Edition (2019). Also available at: https://digitalcommons.law.scu.edu/cgi/viewcontent.cgi?article=2868&context=lawreview

**Criminal Law:**

*The Evolution of Juvenile Justice, From the Book of Leviticus to Parens Patriae: The Next Step After In re Gault*, Loyola Law Review, Volume 53, Number 3, Spring Edition (2020). Also available at: https://digitalcommons.lmu.edu/llr/vol53/iss3/1/

*Children and the Law: Time to Fulfill the Promises of Miranda and Gault*, The Dartmouth Law Journal, Volume 19, Issue 1, Spring Edition (2021). Also available at: https://dartmouthlawjournal.org/article/28217-children-and-the-law-time-to-fulfill-the-promises-of-miranda-and-gault

Website: https://donaldmcinnis.com